SOLDIER *in* PARADISE

Other Books by John Mort

Tanks
The Walnut King and Other Stories

SOLDIER *in* PARADISE

A NOVEL BY JOHN MORT

John Mort (signature)

SOUTHERN METHODIST UNIVERSITY PRESS
Dallas

This novel is a work of fiction. Names, characters, places, and incidents are either the product of the author's imagination or are used fictitiously.

Copyright © 1999 by John Mort
First edition, 1999
All rights reserved

Requests for permission to reproduce material from this work should be sent to:
  Rights and Permissions
  Southern Methodist University Press
  PO Box 750415
  Dallas, Texas 75275-0415

Grateful acknowledgment is made for permission to quote from *Children of God* by Mary Doria Russell, Villard (Random House), copyright 1998.

Chapter Two of *Soldier in Paradise* appeared in somewhat different form as "The Hero" in the New Rivers anthology *Perimeter of Light* (1992). Chapter Nine appeared as the short story "Rest Stop" in *New Letters* and again in the collection *The Walnut King* (Woods Colt, 1990). Elements of the stories "Hot" and "The New Captain," which appeared in the anthology *Missouri Short Fiction* (BkMk, 1985) and in *Missouri Review,* respectively, and were later collected in *Tanks* (BkMk, 1986), appear in Chapter Six. Chapter Fourteen uses elements of a non-fiction reminiscence which appeared in the *St. Petersburg Times*.

Jacket photograph from the Association of History of Ho Chi Minh City

Jacket design by Tom Dawson and Bill Planey
Text design by Bill Planey

Library of Congress Cataloging-in-Publication Data

Mort, John, 1947–
    Soldier in paradise : a novel / by John Mort. — 1st ed.
      p.   cm.
    ISBN 0-87074-440-2 (cloth : alk. paper)
    1. Vietnamese Conflict, 1961–1975 Fiction. 2. Vietnamese Conflict,
1961–1975—Veterans—Florida Fiction. I. Title.
    PS3563.O88163S65   1999
    813'.54—dc21   99-29858

Printed in the United States of America on acid-free paper

10   9   8   7   6   5   4   3   2   1

For my father,
Louis Mort

Pity the poor, wee souls who live a life of watered milk—all blankness and pleasantry—and die nicely asleep in ripe old age.

— Mary Doria Russell,
Children of God

1

There We Were

SOME YEARS AGO, when it was fair, still, to call me a young man, I was invited to an art show in Orlando. It was of the paintings and collages and photographs of a small group of Vietnam veterans. I'm no artist. But I had written a war reminiscence for the newspaper that, for a day or so, brought me a great deal of attention. The veterans thought that I could further their cause.

"Brother," one called me.

It wasn't only veterans who had a need for me. I'd opened the wounds of at least one heartsick woman whose husband was still officially missing in action. What was her name? Deborah Something. Poor Debbie rambled on, almost incoherently at times, as if I were some sort of government priest who could bring her "closure."

What could I say? That her husband, like brave Ulysses, would at last come home? That her husband would be missing throughout eternity? That in all likelihood he'd been blown into so many pieces they couldn't find enough of him to make a memory? This was closure, all right, but I couldn't offer it. All I managed was "Yes, ma'am, I'm so sorry, ma'am," and to fumble my way off the phone.

Then there was that young reporter, Stephanie. She was born about the time that I entered the army, and already had more rungs in her career ladder than I had mounted in all my years on earth. She was innocent and pretty and when she asked if it wasn't painful to talk about Vietnam I said yes. I felt younger when I looked at her. Yes, Stephanie. Quite painful.

She reminded me of what was truly painful: my performance *after* the war. Despite a teaching degree, I hadn't been able to forge a career. I was divorced, which in a roundabout way explained why I'd come to Florida. Worst of all, I hadn't been much of a father to my son, Dale. I left him like a pair of legs in Missouri, and his blue eyes stared back from every mirror.

But as for Vietnam, I'd said in the newspaper what little I had to say. Rather, I'd given up on finding anything to say that hadn't already been said, and with more eloquence than I could muster. My key experiences were those of an infantryman in the time of Homer: boredom and sleeplessness. I seldom knew the day of the week, let alone what campaign I was in, against what regiment. All I knew of politics was to mouth some platitudes.

And yet ... no question ... I was *there*.

Their art took you back to the sixties. It was bold and heroic as if inspired by a John Wayne movie, but it had a shopworn, confusing mysticism as well. In one painting, a unicorn, shrouded in mist, stood on a high bluff, as dying men raised the flag; in another, the Virgin Mary looked down sadly upon a tank battle. In a third, a grunt stood amid smoke and broken bodies and turned his teary face to the rising moon, while Cobra gunships streaked down fiercely, their purple rockets pluming into the blood-red jungle.

There I was, as we said in the old days, at a Holiday Inn in Orlando. The group's leader, called Wombat after his call sign in Vietnam, slapped me on the back and said, "Hey, guy, we need you here."

Wombat had had a little breakdown some years before, and spent time in the Seminole VA hospital. As therapy, he learned to paint, and came roaring back into the world. He formed the artists' group, lining up exhibits at Holiday Inns and malls, and, with the scarcity of artistic venues, a deep-sea fishing trip where his squad took on the roles of rugged outdoorsmen. They'd done some charity work, too, and staked their claim to a mile of Interstate where they picked up trash.

I offered my résumé: the Cav, infantry, some bad shit inside Cambodia, and the heads bobbed approvingly. The men offered a few tales of war but, mostly, I heard tales of peace: like me, these men were lonely, not together because of their art so much as their need for company. I listened to accounts of VA trouble, money trouble, woman trouble. Only Wombat was cheerful; he had a steady job and a marriage that hadn't cracked. He went about slapping backs and issuing comforts, like malaria pills, to his troops.

The universal complaint was that Vietnam veterans were a special category, men to be pitied rather than honored, never on an equal footing with the veterans of World War II or even Korea.

"It's because we lost," I said. "Nobody likes a loser."

The approving faces grew stern.

There was an ex-marine, Dawson, who like me had suffered no serious wounds, or at least none that you could see. He had gone to the war late and was younger than the rest of us, though even he had a sprinkling of gray hair. He was a physical fitness fanatic and as you were talking to him he would muscle up a fist and forearm or bend to touch his toes. He liked to wear his medals, which he had been given for laying down fire as wounded were evacuated, crawling forward, and lobbing grenades, to secure a landing zone. With his Navy Cross, he was our only documented hero.

After a long silence, he offered the group's rebuttal. "The protesters. And worse than that, the politicians. Stood right up in Congress and called us baby-burners."

"We were caught in the middle," I said, wishing that I weren't caught in the middle of this argument.

"We were winning! All they talked about back in the World was Tet, Tet, Tet, but we had the VC with their pants down! Another year the North would have been on its *knees,* man!"

"What for? They're all turning into capitalists over there anyhow. The only difference it would have made, and that's a maybe, is you wouldn't have had Pol Pot, all that Khmer Rouge business."

"Okay. Okay, fucker. How many million did *they* kill?"

"Hey, hey, guy," Wombat said. He was a short man with a full beard, and the beard gave him authority. He grasped Dawson's arms and looked up at him tenderly, as if addressing a child. "Lighten up."

Dawson was actually trembling. He nodded, threw me one hurt glance, and turned away. I was sorry. If I had learned anything through the years, it was to avoid a fight. Yet for me it was a revelation, that some men nurse their wounds not for weeks or even years, but throughout their lives.

We sat all day, and not a single piece of art sold to the sympathetic, but also puzzled and even bemused, public. Good folk paused, as if confronted with a memory, to be nice to these freaks in air force trousers and olive drab headbands. They told stories about someone they knew who'd been in Vietnam and had all sorts of troubles upon his return.

Maybe all veterans groups are pitiful: the vainglory, the half-informed history, the pleas for sympathy. How could you be a hero if you presented yourself as a charity? The truth was that life itself hadn't worked out, and so you concocted a little glory for your youth.

Maybe it wasn't good art. Maybe it was, but who wanted a fleet of Hueys above the mantel?

One man, a Puerto Rican named Otto Sanchez, was a double amputee. Several times during the day, after it had grown clear I wasn't the important contact the group had hoped for, I decided to leave. But instead I stayed, watching Sanchez. He alarmed me in some way I couldn't quite pin down. It wasn't the disability; he reminded me of someone.

It's a nasty thing to say, but I think having Sanchez among us was comforting, because he made it clear how much worse things could be.

He also made our doubts about ourselves the more poignant. We should have won, because Sanchez had no legs.

Surely, life did not offer much for him, but he managed to find his amusements. He donned the expression of an idiot—head cocked a little sideways, vacant stare, tongue lolling—and, index finger pressed on his wheelchair's throttle, went buzzing behind the women. They were saleswomen mostly, bound off to do business with Mickey Mouse. Sanchez brushed under their skirts, within a millimeter of their thighs, and they stumbled forward and turned angrily. Then, seeing he was handicapped, they blushed in confusion.

You could say he was unbalanced, but that's too easy. Perhaps instead Sanchez was calculating, and clever, and cruelly funny. What kind of man turned his body into an insult?

At last we closed up shop, and like the poor men we were took delight eating free from that huge buffet, and staying in a free room. By the pool, no less.

Gene Cooley, whose artistic technique brought to mind those noble roadside renderings of matadors, Harley-Davidsons, and Elvis, unpacked his boom box. He was from some little town in Texas. He had been with an armored unit in the Highlands and was badly burned up one side of his body and face from a freak explosion of C-4. He was a huge man, fat, and he smoked constantly. His life's dream was for the government to declare him one hundred percent disabled, so he'd have enough to live on.

He started a Hendrix tape and settled slowly into his chair. His deep, bloodshot eyes lifted to mine, and I realized I had been staring.

Dawson brought in a cooler of beer, then stood in the corner, not drinking himself, on guard. "Purple *haze*," Hendrix insisted, and Gene Cooley lumbered to his feet again, waved his beer recklessly, jerked in a sort of dance. Panting, he consulted with Wombat concerning the viability of making an attempt on one of the desk clerks. She'd ignored him all day but perhaps her indifference was an act. She was coming on to him.

"Sure, man, go ahead," Wombat said.

We grew loud. Ordinary people, newlyweds and Japanese tourists and salesmen in cheap suits, walked by, stared, but no one complained, and, in any case, the management was inclined to put up with us.

We sank in depression. Any talk about conquering women was only that. It was a world full of enlisted men and officers, and the officers took every fine thing unto themselves. They rode in on white horses, grabbed the good lines, and got the girls in the end.

Gene Cooley hung his head. "I am so fucked up," he said.

Dawson fished out another beer for him. "You're fine, man. Don't talk like that."

"Things gonna turn around for you," Wombat said. "You'll see."

"I *am* fucked up," Gene Cooley said. "The onliest question is whether I am one hundred percent fucked up or just maybe forty percent. I been up before the board three times and I tell 'em I ain't fit to do a goddamn thing, Wombat, but every time they kick the motherfucker out. If I was one hundred percent I could get my own place!"

What a concept, I thought. It was like handicapping a horse. Otto Sanchez, with no legs, was one hundred percent; Gene Cooley, with emphysema, only forty. But wasn't it the spiritual disabilities that dragged you low? What was your average percentage for divorce—all but one of us? What about waiting around all your life for your missing husband? Was working at a terrible job, or not working at all, a disability? Oh, what victims we were, and made of ourselves.

We lived with fathers and mothers and long-suffering sisters, drove old gas guzzlers, ate fast food, smoked generic cigarettes, drank, farted. Could we tell our sons we were heroes when we went to see them on Sundays? What *was* a hero? Was it Dawson, that bundle of nerves who lived in a van out in some swamp, and studied *Soldier of Fortune* like it was the Bible?

I turned again, almost involuntarily, to Sanchez. He favored me with his idiot smile, silent as Harpo Marx. Do I know him? I asked myself. How do I know him?

As though he'd read my thoughts, Sanchez turned his chair and wheeled out the door, across the patio and straight into the pool. The rest of us were so drunk, so sunken in self-pity, that we didn't understand for an instant what Sanchez had done. He's trying to kill himself, I thought. As one, we rushed the door.

"Aw, shit," Gene Cooley said. "Would you look at that?"

We stood alongside the pool and watched that little blob of a man, that morsel of outraged human being, swim.

Not beautifully, perhaps, but he did it.

"He's a tadpole," said Dawson. We all were laughing. What else could we do? We peeled off T-shirts and shoes and jumped in, too; blubbery Gene Cooley was naked. We yelled and screamed obscenities, like that long pool was just another B-52 crater.

The management fished out Sanchez's chair and we plopped him down in it again, covering those obscene-looking plastic stumps with a beach towel. We crowded around our hero, not caring what people thought, how it played. Sanchez looked pale and tired but grinned widely.

It hit me then, who he reminded me of. And I realized, after all my years of silence and rage and blame, that I had something to say.

2

Okie Not Quite from Muskogee

"HERE HE IS, IRISH. Private Norman Sims at the ready."

My God, I thought, and closed my eyes again. It was a little past noon. I'd pulled guard all night and wanted only to sleep, but Hickman had warned me at morning formation that he had a detail for me. In his vocabulary, detail meant punishment.

Hickman was a bald, Old Army black man nearing retirement, and his entire education consisted of army regulations. He'd been giving me trouble because of a little wound I'd taken in my shoulder. Well, not because of the wound, but because I kept finding ways to reopen it and stay in the rear. I knew a soldier in Bravo Company who deliberately contracted gonorrhea to stay out of the field. I wasn't *that* scared.

Norman Sims preempted us both. "First Sergeant, is this man sick?"

"Sappers on the greenline," Hickman grunted. One sapper: we saw him in the Starlight Scope and opened up with an M-60 machine gun. Maybe we got him. "Irish was up all night."

"I understand," Sims said gravely. He stared with bright, sympathetic eyes, and plopped beside me on the bunk.

I jumped to my feet, and with what passed for a smile on that implacable face, Hickman stalked off. Thanks a lot, I thought.

If I had awakened ten minutes earlier, Sims, the fucking new guy, could have been someone else's problem. They were showing *The Good, the Bad, and the Ugly* down at the Filipino compound. I had hoped to make the evening mess and disappear before Hickman mustered guard for the rubber plantation.

On the other hand, I was new once. I'd have been dead several times over if Sergeant Ransom, my platoon sergeant, hadn't taken me under his wing. I tried to smile as I buttoned my shirt. "Where you from in the World, Sims?"

"Oklahoma." Sims stood, too. "How 'bout you?"

"Southern Missouri."

"We're neighbors, I-rish!"

"Right."

He slapped my shoulder—the heroic one—and struck a more intimate tone. "This is it, isn't it?"

I winced and stumbled back. Sims was one of those people who never learn the right distance to maintain from another's face—not that my breath was sweet as apple juice, either. "This is what, new guy?"

"The 'Nam! This is combat." He looked at me eagerly.

"This is a barracks. See the roof over your head, and those bunks? This is getting over, shamming, ghosting, faking it. Marking off *days*, Sims! Combat is out in those mountains."

I studied him, wondering if he had death written all over him, if in five days or five weeks I'd be the one to lay him out in a body bag: Sims, Norman. I couldn't tell. He looked at me with an uneasy arrogance, like a bully who doesn't know his new territory, but also with the shining, simple face of a good dog, all clumsiness and meaning to please.

I went out the door for chow, not caring if he followed—and yet at that I turned, saw his hurt expression, and beckoned. For the moment, he was my responsibility. And, pretty soon, he'd be toting a rifle by my side.

We plodded along. Over the rice paddies and road to the river, a great red dust cloud rolled like a prairie fire. *There we were,* neither the best nor the brightest, a yahoo from Missouri and an Okie not quite from Muskogee, a homesick shit-kicker and a killer at the ready.

"What's your dad do?" I asked.

"I never really knew him. Mom works at the school, she's a cook."

I nodded. "My dad's a truck driver."

"Your mom?"

"A housewife, I guess. When we were on the farm, but she's dead now."

"I'm sorry, Irish!"

I stared. "Thanks. It was three years ago."

Several Vietnamese women, the origin of a soapy stream of water that ran down the eroded red hill, squatted behind the mess hall. They spat betel juice and clucked to one another in a steady whine that became background noise, indistinguishable from Buck Owens, acting naturally on the little radio in the kitchen, and the rumbling of trucks on the road above.

The women were old, but now a younger woman came out the screened back door. She had a broad, unhandsome face, and nothing bulged where her breasts were supposed to be, but her sleek hair hung almost to her waist. We both stared but for all our effect we might have been palm trees.

"Who's she?" Sims asked.

"Just a woman, Sims. Did you want a date?"

He blushed furiously. A gust of wind, full of grit, slammed the mess hall door against the siding, and we ducked inside. I nodded toward the serving line. "The women come from Sông Trì Village. You still have to pull KP, sometimes, but they do the worst of it. Could be that girl's more loyal than Bob Hope. Or could be tonight she gets out that old French Mauser her daddy had, slips under the concertina wire, and blows you away."

"No!" Sims said. Quietly, he added, "She wouldn't do that."

"Well, that's the party line." I shrugged. "They don't like you fooling with the local girls, Sims. It's bad PR and they have to pay the medics overtime, what with all the sickness going around."

He looked unhappy but less skeptical, as if he could tell I was trying to give him the true report. I sat back, munching on a Bartlett pear, watching him. The heat had taken my appetite, but he cleaned his plate and went back.

Soon he was staring at a map that hung in the officers' corner. Colonel Drake did his Robert McNamara imitations there, complete with wire-rimmed glasses and pointer, during staff meetings.

"There are thirty-eight million people in Vietnam," Sims announced.

"We have to go to the rubber plantation tonight. If you need to get laid—"

"I think the Vietnamese women are so pretty," he said quickly. "Wearing their *ao dais*."

I laughed. "The young ladies I'm thinking of aren't quite so formal. They're boom-boom girls, Sims."

"You talk strange, Irish. Boom-boom?"

"'Five dollah one time, twenty dollah all night.'"

He was almost accusatorial. "You make love to these women?"

"Not me." I laughed again. "I'm sworn to another."

"I respect you for that, Irish." He settled back. "I think we all have to remember we're guests here, don't you? We're ambassadors for America, every one of us."

"Right."

"It's like in Oklahoma. I mean you and me, Irish, we're sitting here, we're *white*. You could go with the Indian women, you could give them money, but that didn't make it right. We should honor *all* women! What did Christ do, with the woman at the well?"

Hang around this kid much longer, I'd start going to church.

Toward evening my platoon sat waiting for the deuce-and-a-half that would carry us to the rubber plantation. We hunkered down in the little desert between the Charley and Bravo Company CQs, out of the gritty wind, by a sagging volleyball net. It was February, and chilly enough that several men wore fatigue jackets. Only a hint of winter, and then, rather than spring, interminable summer would be upon us.

Lieutenant Sherry came out to make an inspection. This was routine and he would not accompany us, nor did we want him to. Nonetheless, at least one soldier was sure to bitch about Sherry's absence and the soft life that officers led. The truth was that we'd have a party all night while Sherry patrolled the greenline, watching not for the enemy so much as pot-smokers, sleepers. And, in the field, a second lieutenant's chances of being hit were as high as anyone's.

You saw his sort now and again—in his case, a Harvard man who had come to the war to rub elbows with the folks, then write a book about the experience. If Sherry had been an enlisted man this would have been intolerable, but for an officer it was all right, and we liked him well enough. Officers came and went, after all. Might as well humor them.

Sherry smiled ironically and motioned no, no with his hand when several men acted as though they would line up in formation, as if to say, don't make any fuss on *my* account. Then he looked directly at Sergeant Ransom and me, meaning, bring over the new guy.

Sims came to attention and saluted. After spending the afternoon with him, I wasn't surprised. Ransom, as always, simply took it in. He was an all but illiterate black from Louisiana who didn't curse, smoke, use drugs, or even run down officers. He prayed sometimes, and he played a guitar. He knew Leadbelly tunes such as "Bring a Little Water" and "Ain't Goin' Let You Worry My Life No More."

Ransom saved my life.

Back in September, some fifteen hundred North Vietnamese attacked Bravo Company on Firebase Sheila. After two days they backed off, leaving twenty Bravo men standing, and mounds of their dead in no-man's-land. Charley Company relieved Bravo, drawing the chore of hauling bodies to a long trench the engineers had bulldozed.

I was bending over to grab an upraised arm, a towel clutched to my face to block the stench, when Ransom yanked me back. He shook his head sadly and pointed to a trip wire. If I had lifted the body any further, I'd have pulled the pin on a Chicom grenade, and Sherry would have written a letter to my dad saying I'd died bravely for my country.

"Little things is what get you," Ransom said. "What you don't never expect."

Sims's salute caught the lieutenant off guard, but he hadn't been to school if not for poise. He returned the salute, nodded curtly, and said, "At ease, soldier." He seemed both pleased and suspicious. He threw me a quick look.

Behind us, strung out with cans of soda, radios, and dirty books, the rest of the platoon gawked, and Ransom and I slipped back a little, outclassed for being not quite military enough.

Sherry made it seem like a tea. "Sorry to have missed you this afternoon, Norman. May I call you Norman, by the way?"

"Yes, sir!"

"What do you think of the operation here? I guess it must be rather confusing to you, rather overwhelming."

Sims relaxed. "Yes, sir."

"Everything looks so casual ... so, so *unmilitary.* Don't you think?"

"A little bit, sir. Maybe."

"You probably wish you'd joined the marines. Or gone Air-Borne. Wish you were with the Hundred and Worst, Norman?"

Ransom grinned.

"No, sir," said Sims.

Sherry gave him a long stare, then nodded, as if he'd learned everything about Sims he'd ever need to know. His voice took on the bored tone reserved for orientations everywhere. "Well, no matter how it *looks,* no matter how relaxed it seems, remember one thing. You're carrying a loaded weapon, and it will kill people, or fuck them up bad." Sherry glanced at his watch. "We try to keep safety in mind at all times, and—"

"Here to kill Communists, sir!"

Sherry narrowed his eyes. "You're not bullshitting me, are you, Norman? This gung ho army stuff, is it bullshit?"

"Nosir. You're an officer, sir, and I—"

Sherry smiled. "Fine. Good to have you with us. Maybe you'll teach us a trick or two. You listen to Ransom here; you *watch* him. How many days, Sergeant?"

"One hunnert and forty-seven and a wake-up. Suh."

Sherry grimaced. "The Sergeant liked it here so much he extended his tour, Norman."

Ransom lifted his chin. "I thought it was the right thing, suh."

Sherry nodded. "Of course. Norman, Irish here is a smart-ass, a regular peace advocate, am I right, soldier?"

"Peace with honor!"

The Lieutenant snorted. "Don't listen to him, Norman, he's a good man despite himself. And there's no sweat tonight. Just a little cookout, right, Irish?"

"Roger dodger."

He shook his head. "You might salute me sometime, Irish."

"Yessir."

"Am I your leader, or what?"

"An example for us all, sir."

Not at all in mockery, Sherry smiled and gave the subtle sign—a slightly sterner expression, a more erect posture—that he wanted us to salute. So we did.

"Carry on," he said, and spun about on his toes.

Sims, concluding, perhaps, that ours was some crack garrison unit, spun about, too, and marched down the side of the barracks, sticking out his hand to soldier after soldier. "Private Norman Sims," he said. "From Warner, Oklahoma."

Some of the men smirked. Worm rose, introduced himself as well, and gravely welcomed Sims. Then he withdrew to work painstakingly on a letter to his wife. He was always working on a letter to his wife. Worm was a Mormon. Every day was a challenge to his faith, that the world around him would prove still more evil.

Jim Cole kissed Sims's hand and gave a little bow. He was a Nez Perce from Idaho, a small man with quick movements, wiry, nervous. Sometimes you'd be talking to him and he'd jump to chin himself, or leap up on a table, or flip himself over from a standing position.

And then, alas, there was Dietrich. He was a huge North Dakota farm boy noted for his rages and his intolerance of nearly everything. He'd raped, or almost raped, or statutory raped, some girl at a Holiness baptism service. True enough, she'd been flirting with him, and not delivering, for weeks. Maybe she was worthless, but she was fifteen. Rather than jail, Dietrich was offered a military career.

Dietrich said, "Go fuck thyself, new guy."

Sims nodded happily, as though he would make the attempt.

"Don't mind him, Norman," I said. "It's just *Dietrich*. Let's check your gear."

But Sims marched on. He stepped in front of Detroit, the black machine gunner who was as large as Dietrich but usually more phlegmatic, and said, "Hey, brother!"

Even Ransom raised an eye. "Norman *Sims*," he said. "You sit down."

"Do what?" said Detroit.

"I am sympathetic with you, my brother!"

"Do *what*?"

Sims's head bobbed wildly. "All these college students with their Communist flags? Twenty-two percent of the infantry is black. Ten percent of the country!"

"Oh my Lord," said Detroit. Those reddish eyes of his widened. Was Sims, from ruined Oklahoma, possessed of new information? Detroit shrugged, finally, and turned his head. "My Lord Jesus," he muttered, not acknowledging Sims in any way, except that he was frowning, and his apparent good humor was mock-humor. "Jim Cole, you score today?"

"Yes, I did, big man." As if on cue, Jim Cole began rolling a joint. He poured something green over it from a tiny vial. It made an ojay, an opium-soaked joint named in honor of opium, O. J. Simpson, and orange juice.

C. C. Rider, who got high every morning and did his best to stay that way, smiled hopefully. He'd had two years at the University of Massachusetts and was here only by cosmic accident, which he'd tell you about if he managed to trap you in conversation. Somehow, he'd loped along in the woods and never even been wounded, but I was nervous when he had the point.

I guess Detroit and Jim Cole were trying to shock the new guy, but it was too brazen. Ransom edged away, looking vexed and compromised. Every eye in the platoon fastened on the back of First Sergeant Hickman's head, visible through the window. Worm fidgeted. Dietrich laughed harshly.

"Not *here*, little one." Detroit slapped Jim Cole's back, and the two headed for the latrine.

Sims shouted in my face. "How can they *do* that? It's not right, Irish! Drugs are bad for you and you risk everyone when you use them. Should we tell the Lieutenant? I'm going to tell Lieutenant Sherry. Come on with me, Irish, we'll tell the Lieutenant!"

And he set off to find Sherry. Dietrich came to his feet and I swear he would have decked Sims on principle, but I hurried between them and grabbed Sims's arm. "Calm down, Sims, please. The Lieutenant *knows*."

He dropped into the dirt, his back slamming against the wall of company headquarters. "It's not right," he said. "It's not right."

We rumbled down the red road and through the village. It was light, still, and pleasantly cool. Women who worked on the base stepped through a barbed wire passageway and trudged home. They were shapeless in their baggy black pants and long white blouses, not unlike the women from the shoe factory in my hometown in Missouri.

One or two were younger and prettier and took care not to acknowledge us. Were we trouble?

To be sure. Maybe a soldier can't distinguish virtue from a Claymore mine, but he knows he might die before the night is over. Virtue has no meaning, therefore, but fucking does. A soldier eats, drinks, sleeps, shits, and, if he's a *lucky* soldier, he fucks.

And yet, because of my conversation with Sims, I tried to look at these women differently. Was it my imagination? A beautiful woman came down the path. I could just see her in the tricky light of dusk. Wait, I thought, straining out the back of the truck to catch her eye, don't you hate these charades?

Not beautiful, but merely taller, and when she held up her head her eyes were fierce ... no, her eyes were down. Wait a minute: she wasn't there at all. The truck turned at the shabby crossroads and I looked back where she should be. There were only those plodding, ordinary women.

Sims was getting to me, I thought. I wiped my face with the towel I used to cushion my pack straps, then made a tent of the towel and hid beneath it for an instant, trying to close out the army, trying to think.

Maybe I would write to Cindy. Cindy was a hometown girl, a high school sophomore when I was a senior, thus she was a senior now. She had read in the *Mountain Vale Journal* of my heroic wounds, my subsequent Purple Heart, and it left her swooning.

Or something like that. Cindy went to the same church my mother had, and wrote how much she'd liked Mom and what a shame it was, too, about my father, losing his farm and his wife in the same year. Only faith could bring you through such tragedy, she said, and I must be a very strong person. Nice as she was, I couldn't muster much enthusiasm for Cindy. But no one else had written me, and, lately, she'd been creeping into my thoughts.

The boom-boom girls came from beneath the tin awning of the cafe where they'd sat all afternoon, gossiping and drinking tea. They gathered their gear and mounted their Honda motor scooters as quickly and efficiently as a Special Forces unit. The platoon, looking down at them, variously whooped or assumed the masks of jaded consumers.

A dozen scrawny cows bawled from their pen behind the steam bath, and a boar grunted and waddled off as the truck slowed to ford the shallow creek. We gained speed, bumping and thundering through the rubber trees, with the sun rolling over and over at the ends of rows, a kilometer distant. We'd outpaced the women, and for a moment we seemed significant, manly, even historical.

The driver took us further than usual, to the end of the plantation where the topsoil thinned and the grade rose, so that we looked down upon the river. Ransom said the idea was to watch the woodline on the other shore for enemy movement, for boats, for lights. I smiled at Sims as we climbed from the truck.

"This is the famous Michelin Rubber Plantation!"

Give him an inch. "Part of it, I guess."

"What's the name of that river?"

"I don't know, Sims."

"You don't *know?*"

"Take it easy, dude. You're getting on my nerves."

We set up for the night, Sims and Ransom and Worm and C. C. Rider and me at the high point, looking down into brush and bamboo and a crumbling curve of bluff above the river, Detroit and his gun team twenty feet lower, with the gun aimed toward rubber trees and a roofless stone building that had a permanent, French look about it.

"The French were really cruel," Sims said, beside me again. Could he read my mind? He thought of the French, and so did I. I didn't like it that we were anything similar.

"In the 1930s, when the Viet Minh was starting, the French would go into a village where they knew there was a Communist, *one* Communist, and they wouldn't ask, they wouldn't try to sort out the bad guys, they just waded in with tanks and machine-gunned everything, women and children and livestock, too."

"You're a real fucking scholar, Sims," I said, but I was envious, not knowing even that much.

"Christ, what's the difference?" Dietrich asked. "I don't blame 'em for wading in like that. Maybe some a their guys got wasted the day before. You don't know jackshit, Sims."

"Shhh," said C. C. Rider. "Keep the noise down." Deep in the jungle we had to be quiet, but it didn't matter much here. How C. C. Rider could hear anything, or object to noise, I don't know, since the moment we were set up he plugged into an earphone and sucked down a joint. In the waning light he read from *Siddhartha*.

"We're not like the French," Sims said vaguely, and wandered to the bluff, where he stood, a grand target if anyone from the opposite shore were there to shoot at him. He brought up his rifle and sighted downriver.

"Shithead," said Dietrich. "You better straighten that cherry out, Irish."

"How come it's my job?"

" 'Cause you're the only one in this outfit's got any fucking brains, that's why."

"I'm as dumb as you are, Dietrich."

That shushed him. Ransom brought out his guitar and played the blues for a while, favoring us with his gravelly impression of "Irene." C. C. Rider unplugged his ear, applauded, and offered Ransom some of a new joint, but, of course, Ransom refused.

The boom-boom crew arrived. Detroit and Dietrich went into a thicket for quickies; Dietrich was *very* quick. He dropped under the hooch and said, "Fucking *bitch*."

C. C. Rider attempted a courtship, making jokes the girl didn't understand as she yanked at him impatiently. "You're for peace, right?" he kept saying. He tried to interest her, too, in his joint, but she said, "No, no, hon-eee, number ten!"

Finally, they took a walk by the bluff, unreal, forest creatures in the moonlight. She brought her hands down emphatically and he reached into his billfold for more money. "You got chop-chop?" she asked, and, as if he were running an errand for his mother, he stepped to the hooch and produced some C-ration ham, and cigarettes. "I want to *know* you," he said, as she packed away the cans. "I want to know who you *are*."

Worm, so called because he was tall and everything about him was round, and because he seemed, sometimes, to squirm even sitting motionlessly, successfully fended off Thanh, who was pregnant. He was gentle at first, then angry, as if angry she existed.

Thanh patted her belly. "He have blue eyes."

"Not *me!*"

Finally, Thanh gave up and slipped away to the gun team, where she tried the same argument with Jim Cole. I couldn't recall Worm ever getting laid. I couldn't recall him ever growing angry. He sat squirming.

"The women are crazy for you," I said.

He smiled but didn't reply. He slid under the hooch, pulled up his poncho liner, and lay studying the moon.

No one ever talked to Worm, I thought. He was a Mormon and that was the end of it. "Not much like Utah here."

"Didn't know you'd been there, Irish."

I hadn't. "Sure. My dad loves the West. Zane Grey, Louis L'Amour, like that. Your folks farmers?"

"We have a ranch."

"Really! Raise a lot of cattle? Angus?"

"It's sheep. All sheep."

"Miss it?"

He was so long in answering that I thought he'd fallen asleep. "Sometimes ... in the spring, there's so many lambs, they pen them up all over town. You drive through, there are all these lambs, just *baa-aa-aa-ing*."

"That's nice, Worm. You tell your wife about it, how it is here?"

"Oh, no."

"She'd just be upset."

"That's what I thought, and—"

"You're doing good, Worm. You'll be fine."

There was little need for caution because we knew that nothing would happen. Our orders might be to observe the river but, in truth, Colonel Drake didn't want us on the base at night, when we tended not to behave well. More: the women were barometers. If there had been enemy in the area they would have known, and stayed home from the party.

Some party, I thought, rolling over, laying my head in the grass.

C. C. Rider's girl approached Sims. "The Bible says—," he began, and the woman backed away.

Dear Mom: having a great time but it's really hard to meet people.

Oh, Mom. I saw her in the hospital bed, so worn-down, so frail, and closed my eyes. The night was cool, and, far below, the river ran soothingly. Dream of the river, I told myself. Think of that cold spring in the mountains where it began, of clear water falling over stones. Think of the river's long course to the Mekong.

I sat upright. A round went off and there was a scream. "I-rish! Oh God, Irish!"

I grabbed my rifle and crawled forward. I looked down at the moon on the water and the trees on the far shore, that land beyond the bridge where the North Vietnamese were camping, Indian Country. Sims lay moaning.

"Chickenshit cherry," Dietrich said. "Scared a the fucking moon." He made a move as if to kick Sims. I jumped on his back, and Ransom, half his size, drew him to one side. "What you *mean,* boy? Man hurt!"

"One day in-country, he shoots hisself," said Jim Cole.

"Fucking slick, you ast me." Detroit bent over Sims, cutting away his boot. I held Sims's arms. He jerked back, whimpering, though Detroit was careful, I thought, even tender.

"They'll come after you now, Norman," I said. "Shoot your foot back in the World, not here."

"It was an accident!" Sims moaned.

Soon the Medevac churned in the moonlight. The nose of the bird lifted high as its light shone down. Jim Cole popped a flare and yellow smoke swirled under the rotor blades.

The boom-boom girls huddled. Some of them climbed onto their Hondas.

"Norman Sims," Ransom said. "You in a world a hurt."

After he shot his foot Sims became a nonperson. If he tried to join a group of us in from the field, sitting at mess, no one answered when he spoke, and one by one rose to leave. Resident shammers avoided him, for, as I could testify, there was honor even among malingerers. You were faking it because, once upon a time, you had been wounded, or your body was so cut and pussy from jungle rot you could hardly wear clothing.

To shoot yourself in the foot was at best the most amateurish and clumsy thing a soldier could do, and, at worst, it was cowardly. What was an infantryman if he couldn't handle his rifle? Deny it every day, swear it was an accident, and it would always seem, nonetheless, that you had done it purposefully. It would have been more honorable to refuse a direct order or frag battalion headquarters. It would have been more honorable to have sweated out time in Long Binh Jail.

First Sergeant Hickman made jokes about Sims at morning formation. "How's our *girl* today?" he'd ask. "He so scared a Charley, Charley don't even have to fire his weapon. Man shoot hisself!"

The shammers were quick to laugh, because it took the pressure off each of them. And Sims was easy to despise because he had no defiance in him. The more you ridiculed him the more sensitive he became: his whole body shook, not from fear, but woe, and the feeling he'd let his country down.

Hickman had him burn shit unless he could conjure a worse detail. When I'd drawn it, I'd sit away from the smoke, read something long and irrelevant such as *Bleak House,* and make the best of things: digging drains or filling sandbags were more strenuous duties. But if you were told to burn shit day after day it was a way of shaming you. It was a way of saying that you were an untouchable, shit yourself.

Except that poor Sims didn't get the message. I'd see him hobbling on his cast, lugging out the heavy half-barrels and pouring in diesel fuel. He'd wave cheerfully as he bobbed through the foul black smoke, stirring each tub with a hoe. They also serve? Once I heard him singing "Val-de-ri ... Val-de-ra ..."

When Sims had finished he'd ask Hickman for more work. Amazed, Hickman would tell him to sweep company headquarters, and then Sims would try to engage Hickman in patriotic talk. Sims would ask this aging, wifeless, Regular Army, old school enlisted man about the dedication of the North Vietnamese, contrasting it with the relaxed attitudes of the Thais and Filipinos, who appeared simply to be *mercenaries.* How could such a thing be?

Why were we fighting, in First Sergeant's opinion? Sims believed in the war, certainly, but he'd seen some things that didn't add up. Could First Sergeant explain why there was so much drug use?

Worse: had First Sergeant's career been a rewarding one, and would he recommend it to a young person? Wasn't it a lot easier for black people than it had been? Was First Sergeant a member of one of those famous black companies in France, way back in World War II? What did you have to do, Sims wanted to know, to be nominated for Soldier of the Month?

Pretty soon Hickman must have sensed that Sims had indeed shot himself accidentally. It made him seem like more of a clown, but of a sort the First Sergeant could recognize. In those days, the army was renowned for its ability to provide a home for the man who, in civilian life, couldn't find a girl, hold a job, or keep a car on the road. Despite himself, First Sergeant may even have begun to *like* Sims.

But he was such a pest, even so, that Hickman ordered him from the company headquarters and to the Red Cross Club. Go to the movies! Play idiot games with the Doughnut Dollies! Let an old man *be,* boy!

Finally, he assigned Sims to KP. "Until I come and get you," he said. Now he wouldn't even have to look at him. Sims was up before dawn and didn't quit until late afternoon.

That was when Sims fell in love.

He fell in love with the woman he'd asked me about his first day in-country. Her name was Cuc Hoa and their shared vocabulary, English and Vietnamese and, perhaps, some French, couldn't have totaled two hundred words. I'd hear her call his name, in a high voice, "Nor-*mahn!*" And he'd call hers, slurring it, so it sounded like "Cowkie." Norman and Cowkie, dream couple.

For a while, I was the only one to notice. He was no hero, remember, hardly a soldier at all, not to be noticed unless he pounded on your door. I'd stand on the road above the mess hall, watching them, amazed.

They sat opposite each other over a pot of vegetables and she fed him a bit of potato. He took it from her fingers with his teeth and she reeled in laughter. The crones laughed, too. He'd go among them, call them each by name, by their real names rather than their made-up American names. He'd shake his finger in mock anger. He'd pick up a banana and leap about on his cast, knuckles dragging the cement. Laughter pealed down the hill.

He carried their heavy pots. He hobbled down the hill and returned with iced Cokes. He spent half a day rigging a parachute for shade, and from somewhere produced chairs and wooden ammunition crates, to make a sort of table. The old women still sat on their haunches but Cuc Hoa and Sims sat at the table, saying sweetly whatever it was they said, delicate shadows fluttering over them in a kind of parody of the colonial French, say, at a Saigon cafe. One day she made him tea and served it in dainty Japanese cups.

Sometimes, still, he drew latrine duty. So he must have had an evil smell about him, of shit and diesel fuel. Once, I saw her pinch her nose, hold high her head, march haughtily away. Sims peeled off his shirt to wash. She came behind, and ran her hands across his back.

It was a revelation. If I imagined that all the world was an army camp, and whether you were in the army of good guys or bad guys some men were lowest of the low and had to burn shit—well, there would still be women to love them.

I did a strange thing. What, after all, were the odds of someone like Norman Sims finding true love in the middle of war, as he pulled KP and was shunned by every fellow soldier? As if the filthy base were the campus of the little college I'd attended, I sought that girl I'd seen walking in the twilight weeks before.

Not quite every woman in my young life had been imaginary. Besides Cindy, there was Trudy from my one and only year of college.

She was a tall, thin pacifist who played the organ for religious assemblies, and played the guitar and sang Bob Dylan songs when we were alone. She convinced me that I, too, was a pacifist, and she never forgave me for going to war.

I tried not to think of Trudy, but sometimes she invaded my dreams. I thought of her as I pulled guard, and it was almost more than I could bear. I made her into the most beautiful girl in the world when, truthfully, she was plain—fiercely so, since she refused to wear makeup or jewelry.

I'd visualize her long legs, her tiny breasts, the way her ears pointed out of her limp brown hair, and how limber she was, pointing her toes heavenward as I fumbled my way inside her, not quite certain of the coordinates.

In moments she'd hammer at my chest until I rolled over. Then she'd climb on top, where she hunched her knees into my belly like I was a horse, and cried out nonsense, and yanked at my hair. At such moments I doubt if she knew my name, but she made me dizzy, even so, and I was dizzy thinking about her ten thousand miles away, because she was the only real girlfriend I'd had. Then in the absolute darkness, with a supreme act of will, I'd cast her from my mind almost in hatred.

Still, I spent half a day wandering from the Filipino compound to the PX to the Red Cross Club. Apparently, my imaginary woman worked on the base. Where?

I'd plucked her from a romance of Vietnam, from picture books with Vietnamese/French girls walking the sidewalks of civilized Hue, and mixed her with my suppressed longings for Trudy. Vapors. Such a woman didn't exist, just as Trudy didn't exist unless I allowed her to.

Sims and Cuc Hoa were absurd. Sims was insane. I decided I preferred my own company and every morning, as soon as I could, withdrew to a quiet corner at the Red Cross Club, and read Dickens, and slept. When we were ordered to the field again, I was almost grateful.

Late in March Sims's cast was removed. He reported to First Sergeant Hickman immediately, announcing he wanted to go to the field and kill Communists. I can't say how he broke the news to Cowkie, if she kissed him good-bye and swore she'd be true.

Hickman delayed for a day or two. He tried to palm Sims off on the new first sergeant in Bravo Company—a poetic gesture, since they were the battalion's hard luck company. Bravo needed men, and sometimes in the past soldiers had been exchanged with Charley, but the new first sergeant was from Decatur, Alabama. He wasn't convinced blacks belonged in the army at all, and it made him more uncomfortable, still, that one had attained his own rank and pay. So he asked around about Sims and got the true report.

No, thank you, he said.

We were in the mountains when Sims rejoined us. We'd had light contact every day for three weeks, killing four and five at a time. We'd lie quietly at midday, near water like deer hunters, and blow them away. They were spooky, small men who wore pith helmets with leaves stuck in them, and tied branches to their packs. You'd wait, wait, nearly die in the thought that momentarily you would have murdered someone, and then you'd snap the Claymore trigger. *Boom! Boom! Boom!* Go find the pieces.

As the bird landed Sims was leaning across the small distance within, trying to talk to the chaplain. The chaplain bit on his cigar, the muscles in his cheeks hardened, but his lips didn't move, and, when the struts touched down, he stalked quickly away.

Sims hung in the clearing, looking sheepish. Another bird arrived immediately and, without being prompted, he unloaded the water, but he made no move to load the two bodies lying wrapped in camouflage covers. No one touched them until the chaplain was ready to fly out again, when he and Sims, without speaking, their eyes cast away to the treelines, loaded them. Then the chaplain gave thumbs up, the bird lifted away, and Sims sat on the water cans, looking nervous.

Finally, Lieutenant Sherry called me to his position. I was first squad leader by then, heir apparent to Ransom as platoon sergeant. "You have to take him, Irish. Nobody else will."

"Lonely Platoon's short an ammo-bearer."

"They know he's a fuck-up. The word is, if he shoots himself accidentally, or if he shoots himself on purpose, either way he's a fuck-up." The Lieutenant smiled. "But he likes *you.*"

I shrugged. "I'm not sure. I mean, if he's a fuck-up. I think— I think he's a patriot, sir."

A helicopter took off and the Lieutenant's short hair fluttered a little. He laughed. "We're all patriots here, aren't we, Irish?"

"I think of Mom and apple pie, and I go dead inside."

Sherry grunted. "You teach him not to fuck up, maybe he can teach you to be a patriot." He dropped three Tootsie Rolls into my hand.

"Sir?"

"My girlfriend sends them. It's what kept Aldo Ray going, Irish, in all those war movies. Must have been."

"I'll look after Norman, sir."

"I know you will."

Sometimes, I'd wake with Sims's arm across my neck. I'd nudge him and he'd roll over into Jim Cole. Jim Cole swore mildly, but, if anything, he was sorry for Sims, and offered him favors through the day: a piece of gum, a can of V-8 his wife had sent.

Detroit eyed him with a kind of fatherly indifference, as though Sims wasn't important enough to get excited about one way or the other. Subtly, Sims had come to be seen as bad luck, but merely his own bad luck.

Even Dietrich said nothing.

Sims kept to himself, except once or twice he attempted a religious discussion with Worm, who, offended, quickly withdrew when Norman told him that the *Book of Mormon* was false prophecy. No doubt Worm put it down in a letter to his wife.

Ransom let Sims be. He seemed wearier now, more withdrawn, intent at last on making it home. A woman from his church had been writing him. I'd see him off by himself with her letters, piecing them out slowly and looking embarrassed, too proud to ask me to read them.

The Lieutenant came over in the mornings, map in one hand, coffee in the other. He always shaved first thing and it made him look young, like Audie Murphy rather than Aldo Ray. "Are you okay, Norman?"

"Yessir!"

"Got that weapon squared away?"

Sims looked mournful. "Yessir. I'm really thankful you gave me another chance. It was an accident, and I—"

"No, no." The Lieutenant swallowed coffee and lowered his eyes, suppressing a smile.

Another chance? Was that what it was?

*   *   *

The company zigzagged along the mountain, gradually climbing. Sims pounded tree trunks and looked up as if measuring for a log. He stared off at birds, stopped, listened carefully. He plucked flowers and tasted the petals. And he had a glow about him, sometimes, a pleasant, faraway look.

"You thinking about your girlfriend?" I asked.

"She's so nice."

"You can't marry them, you know. They put you through hell."

"I can marry who I want to!"

We drew the point every six or seven days, and, in the meantime, I tried to show Sims the simple things, such as how to read a compass and sight an azimuth on a far tree. The art of pointing wasn't really an art. It required endurance, and nerve, and brute force as you tore your way through vines and chopped at low-hanging limbs.

Even so, there were days when the world became subtler, when it was easy to die and take men with you. The distance ahead ebbed in warning. You listened for sounds not otherwise a part of things, not akin to the steady tramping of boots far behind, the fall of branches, water dripping from the great, umbrella-like air plants. You looked for a violated logic in the way the grass grew or the vines hung, bruised, around the trunks of trees. To the left a tall weed was broken, and not by a bird. Suddenly, a rat was running. Did it feed on rice?

The other two platoons were apprehensive at first, because point men walked with their weapons off safety. They eyed Sims strangely, not as if he were an enemy but a dubious ally, such as a South Vietnamese.

But if Sims had a problem it was that he took me too literally and was too cautious, stooping to investigate every least indentation in the earth. He called for me and the file was delayed and then Captain Keel complained. Sherry ducked his head from the leaves and motioned urgently.

"Listen," Sims said.

"What, man? What now?"

"Do you hear the birds, Irish? They don't sound right. Do you think they sound right?"

I laughed. "It's when you *don't* hear them, Sims."

It was a nameless river our maps hadn't shown, and the sound of its running, between a bluff on one side, the jungle and flat tiers of stone on the other, echoed off the rock and was absorbed by the wall of trees and vines. The roar seemed solid, like a barricade; the river wasn't fifteen meters wide but its force charged the air. A cool energy rose with the river's mist, and I recalled an emotion I once had known well: joy.

The men milled in a tight, grassy clearing by the rock shore, and began shouting, in wonder at the river and confusion how we'd cross. There was a tall, skinny tree loaded with what seemed to be figs, and one man from Lonely Platoon began climbing it, until Captain Keel emerged from the jungle and ordered him down. Keel placed the gun positions, and spaced the rest of us along the sloping jungle side of the bluff, but still it seemed like a holiday. Men settled against their packs and ate lunch.

Keel and Lieutenant Sherry stood by the water and talked. The Lieutenant broached a scheme he'd learned in Panama at survival school, and Keel seemed doubtful, but it was ritual doubt.

Keel was new, from a National Guard unit in upstate New York, and had volunteered for Vietnam because of his disgust with the Communist sympathizers who were everywhere in America now. Heartbreaking, how the country had deteriorated. He was in his late thirties and would probably never even make major, at least not in the real army, and so a notion from Sherry, the Harvard man, was automatically suspect. But he didn't have a better idea.

Up high, the triple canopy grew together, meshing like spread fingers, hints of blue behind. Jim Cole, our acrobat, climbed with a coil of rope around his shoulders, and walked out a limb near the sky. He bent it and scrambled to a tree on the opposite side, dropped like a lineman coming down a pole, and secured the rope. Sherry brought the rope down on our side, looped it, knotted it, tossed it to Jim Cole again. Jim Cole tied it off, and now there was a rope for your feet inches over the water, and one above that to cling to.

Sherry glanced toward Keel, looking pleased with himself. Jim Cole beat on his chest and let out a Tarzan yell, or maybe it was a Nez Perce war cry. You couldn't hear it above the river's roar. But the men cheered, and Captain Keel nodded irritably, and we were in business.

It seemed like an adventure, like a film of the war, with the brown water gushing beneath each soldier's feet, the rope careening wildly, all in jungle so dense you couldn't see one hundred meters upstream or down. Aldo Ray should have been there, barking orders.

The men sprawled awaiting their turns, while those who had crossed called back that the water was fine. Most of Lonely Platoon made it over, and Dietrich and Worm, and Lieutenant Sherry. Sims went gaily across like it was some playground trick.

Ransom made a good start but the bottom rope veered away, and he lost his footing. I had never seen him look fearful, never seen his mask of calm drop. "He can't swim," said Detroit, and we edged to the shore, shouting, "You can make it!"

Lonely Platoon was laughing at him and his outrage at their laughter cut visibly into his fear, but even as his feet steadied he went off the bridge on the upstream side, and lost most of his gear. He clutched at the line and managed somehow to hold his rifle above water. I got on the rope, wanting to help, but his eyes rolled at the surface, caught mine, and I stopped.

He was all right. Sherry leaned out as far as he could, one foot on a rock shelf beneath the surface, one hand steadying the rope, and Ransom pulled along and took the Lieutenant's hand. He drew to land and hunched over, coughing. Sherry bent near, but Ransom shook his head and brought up one knee, leaned on his rifle like a walking stick. He nodded and looked upstream, his eyes blood-red.

C. C. Rider crossed, carrying the gun, looping it to the high rope and sliding it along. He crawled out and threaded his way through the vines, sinking down by a log up the shore.

The sun weakened; light seemed to fade all around me. The water felt colder. I looked up again from the river rushing under me and C. C. Rider was eating a can of peaches, staring. He called out something to Dietrich, who didn't reply.

Beyond him Lonely was stretched out, some of them asleep. It had been almost two hours since we reached the river. Not quite half of us were across.

Ransom smiled gravely. Sims said, "C'mon, Irish!"

In the middle my boots went under water. Detroit hung back until I was rising again, and then walked quickly out ten feet or so. "Feel *good*," he said, and I said, "What?" and their machine gun opened up.

Detroit and I should have been killed instantly. But they raked the shore where Lonely lay and both of us dropped into the water. We hung helplessly, our gear and weapons gone, the current sweeping around us.

Captain Keel stepped to the river's edge, his back springing erect, but he could not have seen anything but the men of Lonely, diving for cover. He and the men with him dropped low, too, but they were never in danger. The gun was on their side but the stream curved above, blocking off the enemy. In seconds, Keel realized that. He screamed into the radio, but Lonely's operator was dead.

From the water I could see men jumping crazily, rolling over, taking hits, frantically scurrying backward for a rock or body to hide behind. Rounds peppered the water ahead of me.

I imagined a cleft in the rock. A cave? The fire angled downstream and zipped along the shore and I dropped senselessly underwater. I rose, choking, feeling stupid and afraid.

Detroit screamed at C. C. Rider to get the gun going, but C. C. Rider had rolled down by the water. He lay there now, eyes wide. He brought a thumb to his chest and his lips said, "Me? You mean *me*?"

"Go, go!" Detroit screamed. And C. C. Rider tried once to crawl forward, but the firing kept on and he couldn't bring himself to do it. He hunched up on his knuckles, then dropped again.

"Go, go!" Detroit yelled.

Sherry leaped up with a grenade but the firing turned instantly his way, and he dropped. He crawled forward slowly, flat on his belly, trying himself to reach C.C. Rider's gun. He slid near the water by a massive tree root, and dropped from sight.

Dietrich and Worm crouched behind a log, making no effort to rise in the withering fire.

Ransom lay bleeding. On the safe side, Keel and his men would have seen nothing but the wounded black man, hand clutching his thigh, head thrown back, mouth open. They could not have heard him screaming. "Lord Jesus, let me go. Let me go, let me go home, Jesus!"

The Captain shook his fist at me and pointed to his radio. "Cobra! Cobra!" I thought he said. Up there? I tilted my head in the water and couldn't see anything through the leaves. But he wanted me on a radio, wanted me to call in the Cobra. God, a run from a gunship was futile, more dangerous for us than them. I slid along the rope, trying to stretch out a foot and find the rock beneath. I'd have to roll over Ransom.

"Where the hell's Sherry?" I screamed.

Detroit made it back. He stood talking to the Captain, who nodded furiously. Detroit moved around the bluff with half a dozen men.

The Captain glared and somehow I was moving, hand over hand, weaponless, until my feet hit the rock below. Their gun was going but not at me. I'd make a leap, and roll. *Now!*

I might have made it. I might have done something to make a difference, but as I was about to leap Norman Sims stood and ran to the gun. There was no pause in the firing and he should have been killed, but he wasn't. It was almost as though certain death was not an idea he understood. Sims dropped to his belly, turned the gun around, propped the barrel across a dead man. C. C. Rider lay open-mouthed, watching him almost disapprovingly.

Sims made the gun roar, and quickly the survivors in Lonely rallied with their rifles. I could hear both machine guns for a while, a duel, but Ransom inched forward to feed belts of ammunition, and everyone screamed at Sims to keep it up.

No need: he was so cool, so fearless, that it was as though by pure conviction he would not allow any more men to die. In some strange way Sims wasn't shooting at real men, but at the Communists he'd heard about since grade school. There was hatred on his face, and mercilessness, and a kind of evil, war movie sneer.

I crawled ashore and gathered boxes of ammunition and threw them forward. A branch jabbed into my shoulder and threw me back. All my arm felt hot.

Ransom shouted at Sims, "There! There!"

He never paused. Under the cover of his fire, I slipped into the woods and ran forward, to emerge on the water thirty meters upstream. I crawled, coming to my knees with a grenade poised. From the new angle I could see them, five men, all dead behind that terrible gun. A path ran upstream and another man lay dead across it.

A new face poked from above, far across the river: Detroit. He looked down at me as if I were a stranger. He dropped a grenade before I could wave him off. I saw the bodies coming apart as I ducked, pieces hissing into the river and splattering onto the rock behind. A boot and foot sailed high and landed in front of Sims.

Ransom lay with his eyes closed. I yelled at Sims and he stared at me, nodded, ceased firing. His eyes rolled upward. He crossed his hands over his crotch and went pale. "Irish," he said. "I-rish."

Men came from the other side. The Captain looked at Sims and Ransom and licked his lips. He leaned down to touch Ransom's arm. "You'll make it," he said. "Dustoff's coming."

The Captain looked at me. "Okay, Jonesy?"

"Name's Donnelly, sir. What?"

"You're bleeding, Jonesy."

"I—" I couldn't remember how it happened. I'd taken a round through my shoulder again, through the very scar of my wound. Now I felt the pain shoot through my chest and my arm went limp. I sat heavily, all the way down to the grass.

"Where—?" Captain Keel was leaning over. He held the Lieutenant's head so that he seemed to stare at me.

"Christ," the Captain said. He knelt and looked Sherry in the eye, as if there were still something to say or do. "Barely knew the man. You know him, Jonesy?"

"Sir, I—"

"I had to do it." Sims was blubbering. "Everybody was going to die! So I had to do it, it was us or them. I saved us!"

"You're a brave man, soldier," said the Captain. He dragged the Lieutenant up against an anthill, and stood looking around the smashed jungle, and nodding, as though he'd encountered a profound truth.

Sims grinned. He ran back and forth. "I'm a brave man," he said. "I'm a hero!"

"Easy," I said, rising slowly, the pain in my arm flooding over me. I reached for Sims but he shoved me away. I hadn't known how strong he was. I had to sit again. I stared at Lieutenant Sherry. I didn't understand how he could be dead.

Sims walked by the river, peering across at the dead men. He grew quiet. Slowly, he drew himself to attention. Then he fell, as if there were no strength left in his legs, and lay giggling.

3

Soldier in Paradise

WHEN I HAD BEEN in Florida for six months I had a call from Billy Harpster, my neighbor back in Missouri. I'd broken the land into three parcels when I sold my farm, and he bought one. In fact, his payments constituted my child support for a while, and I was worried he'd inform me that he was declaring bankruptcy or some such, since he and his family were always struggling.

Billy told me that my house had burned down. Not mine anymore, of course.

The man who bought it was a foundry worker about my age, Bob Kohler. He had a new wife, hardly twenty years old, and a baby daughter. It was the kind of situation about which you'd say at a glance, "That won't last," but the bank didn't think so. Kohler's credit was fine, it seemed, and my interests ended there.

His wife liked my kitchen. After Cindy left, and without my son, Dale, underfoot, I had plenty of time to finish it. The original house was a classic Ozark story-and-a-half. But it was built in the 1920s, and the lean-to for the bath and kitchen that went up thirty years later was strictly Dogpatch. I tore off the lean-to and cooked with a microwave, pissed in the yard. My father's son.

Billy Harpster helped me hoist the rafters, but I pounded the nails into every stick afterwards, and strung the wires, and slapped up the ceiling. Oh, you should have seen me, propping up the far end of an eight-foot piece of sheetrock with a furring strip, pushing up the near end with my thick skull, balancing on one foot at the top of the ladder as I reached out with hammer and nail.

I laid the drains and water lines, installed the sink and dishwasher. I picked out the prettiest vinyl wallpaper and no-wax tile. I should have given *Better Homes & Gardens* a ring.

There I was, idiot ex-husband in his utility belt, building the American Dream kitchen for the bird who had flown. If that's not heroism, what is?

I was weird after Cindy left. I was weird before or she wouldn't have left, but let that go for a moment.

At first, Cindy had every intention of returning. She wanted me to say, "Let's sell the place, we're not farmers," and for me to hold a steady job. I didn't *want* her back. I was a tortured genius, a mad monk bent on finishing a project nobody cared about anymore. I cranked up Creedence Clearwater Revival to five million decibels and sucked down a joint and laid floor tile. I *had* to. What little pride I had remaining was bound into it, nor was the house worth much unless I finished.

As for how I was weird before, I liked to say that it had nothing to do with the war. And true enough, I didn't have flashes of combat, and my nightmares were infrequent. Sometimes, if you woke me suddenly, I'd jump as if to strike you, but even that passed after a while. Smoking marijuana as I finished the house was an aberration.

I seldom talked about the war, and it took a trip to Florida for me to think about it much. But it isn't quite true that my reminiscence in the newspaper was all that I had ever wanted to say about Vietnam. I had wanted to be a writer, and as Cindy and I were finishing college, I'd even published a few short stories in places where nobody noticed. It mystified me at the time. I thought there'd be offers from Hollywood.

I spent weeks, months, years, turning out my mediocre stories and diddling along in a novel, instead of—well, working on the kitchen. I couldn't settle down to an ordinary job because I was convinced I was extraordinary. History remembers the eccentric geniuses who succeeded. You never hear from the ones who merely *imagined* that they were geniuses.

Bad enough, but I'm not sure that was the true effect Vietnam had on me. Even hillbillies have dreams, after all, if only of a gorgeous wife and a new John Deere.

No, if I have anything to blame on Vietnam, it's that I lost respect for authority. There was a son of a bitch calling the shots at every job I held: in schools, until my displays of anger got me fired; in the furniture factory, where I thought the work was beneath my dignity, and quit; and in one convenience store, where I tried desperately to succeed but was accused, falsely, of slipping twenties from the till, and was fired.

Every boss I had was that idiot supply sergeant in Bien Hoa, or maybe a congressman calling me a criminal for doing what he'd told me to do. And I'd never learned, not from Vietnam, not even from my humbled father, to drop my head and shuffle. Fuck you, I'd say, I don't have to *take* this. I was smart enough, talented enough. But when I'd seem to be doing well I'd imagine that my boss was plotting against me, confront him with wild accusations, and quit. Or, God knows, I'd have a real grievance, and quit. I punched one guy, and quit. He threatened to take me to court.

There were so many jobs I can't remember them all. Seventeen, was it, in twelve years? Was it Vietnam, or the paranoia coded in my DNA? Finally, when Dale was born, and when it seemed doubtful I could even *find* another job, Cindy and I agreed that I'd stay home, cook, and take care of the baby—the house-husband arrangement that never seems to work.

Cindy's career had taken off, more from steadiness and hard work than brilliance, and it grew harder for her to tolerate my wounded psyche. She couldn't, you know, take me anywhere.

"What do you do, Mr. Donnelly?"

"I fail."

The country life wore thin. What was I doing, mimicking my ineffective father? I planted four hundred peach trees, two hundred of which died. I bought an ancient Allis-Chalmers which, I concluded, had been *designed* not to run. I tried pigs, cattle, corn, and lost money on them all.

Cindy's money.

I exploded at the dinner table. I threw dishes at the bare studs of the walls and food on the particleboard floors and screamed why was it that a genius like me had to sit at home and change diapers?

"You want to write," Cindy said.

"I *can't* write! I'm no damn good!" This was clever, I must say. It showed that I had *some* talent as a writer, if I could trade for sympathy on my lack of talent. Cindy was supposed to say that I was a genius but that the system was against me. I had to keep at it like all those great writers in the past had.

Unfortunately, she'd said this a number of times already. And what she said now was, "Then get a job, Patrick."

"I *had* a job. That bastard Carson—"

"And hold onto it." After which Cindy put on her lawyer duds and marched off to the courthouse, where she saw to it that characters like me got psychiatric help.

Two months after I sold him the place, Bob Kohler lost his job. His wife moved out. Then *he* moved out and stopped making mortgage payments.

One night at three in the morning he drove to the farm and loaded his pickup with furniture. He shut off the water at the pump and closed all the windows. Then he walked through my kitchen splashing gasoline on my no-wax tile. There were no fire-stops between the floors in that old house. It was ashes in ten minutes flat.

Everyone knew he'd burned it down. They even threw him in jail for a while. But the local arson investigator couldn't agree with the one from the state on the precise chain of events, and the insurance investigator had a different story still, and our friend from the foundry had hired a clever lawyer.

I worked ten years on that house, and after Cindy got her share and the debts were paid, took away enough for a used Volvo and the deposit on my apartment in St. Petersburg.

Bob Kohler torched the place and made enough for a brand-new home.

When I was a boy my father, tough old George Donnelly, would talk of Florida as though it were Paradise. All the people in Florida had sunny dispositions, the fishing was good, and the oranges and figs and strawberries were the best on earth. In the coldest days of winter, when we had to break ice for the stock and haul wood through the snow, or dig out a frozen pipe or start a balky tractor, it was easy to believe him.

It may be, at mid-life when my luck ran out, that I came to St. Petersburg because of him. Though he had been dead almost ten years and we had barely spoken for ten years before that, still I would take his advice.

Secretly, I thought that in Florida I would be young again, that the years since Vietnam would dissolve into dreams. I would make a killing in real estate, go adventuring among the Seminoles, don a golden tan.

Not quite. I rented an apartment in the poorest section of town and worked at two separate, and separately dead-end, jobs. I drove that wheezing Volvo, ate TV dinners and peanut butter sandwiches, and before long, while I did save some money, any distinction between myself and animals had blurred.

On the other hand, I didn't quit.

When Dale came at Christmas it was a day and more until I could remember who I had been, in the role of his father. He was nine then. He looked up at me with those blue eyes and I didn't know what he saw. I could not take him among my friends or show him where I worked, because I had no friends and at work I was a robot.

Then, together, we discovered the Florida my father must have been thinking of. We picked tangerines over a fence, rode bicycles by the bay, and Dale caught a fish. We befriended a big cormorant that had wrapped itself in thirty-pound line.

We went to the zoo in Tampa's Lowry Park, to the beach, to Sunken Gardens. We drove to the Space Museum near Cape

Canaveral, and, next day, stood by the Indian River to watch a shuttle launch.

We went to Disney World. We played basketball.

"You're really good, Dad."

"No. I'm just tall."

"Did you play a lot when you were a kid?"

"I had a goal out on the barn but I never learned to dribble. Dad thought sports were foolish. He always made me work."

"Did he pay you?"

"No way."

"Mom pays me for chores. Was Grandpa a good farmer?"

"Not so good, I think. It was just a hill farm; he didn't have much to work with. There was a drought, Mom died, everything went to pieces. He had to sell out and move to town."

"How did he die?"

I paused. "He just … died. I went down to see them, sometimes, before you were born. We didn't get along that well, but every once in a while we'd try to bury the hatchet. I remember going along—with him and his wife, Mavis—to get groceries, and we were talking about the war and he was *trying* to say he was proud of me. He had an old Studebaker he'd fixed up, he was proud of that, too.

"But then some black kids went across the street, they had these silly pink combs in their hair, and that set him off. He said 'nigger' and it drove me crazy. I was with all those black guys in Vietnam, you know. I said, 'Why aren't you sympathetic? You never had any money, either.' Mavis—I swear, Dale, the woman is a saint—she said, 'Stop it, stop it, I can't take it anymore.' And—"

"Mavis said that?"

"You know Mavis?"

"She and Mom go out for lunch, sometimes. She always gives me ten dollars."

"Really." I swallowed. "Anyhow, she and I went in to get groceries, and she said, 'He's your father, you've got to be patient with him,' and I told her I'd try, and then we came out and he was just sitting there, behind the wheel in the Studebaker, he'd been reading a western. He loved those westerns. We took him to the hospital but he was gone in three days. I remember shaking him. I thought he was asleep."

"He *died?*"

"He had a heart attack. We didn't even know he was sick, because he hid it, kept driving that truck ... he'd had a lot of trouble. Money troubles, I didn't *know,* Dale."

Dale seemed to consider. "Dad, will you do me a favor?"

"Sure."

"When we go to a supermarket, you come in, too."

I laughed, and understood all over again that I had to climb to my feet for his sake, if not my own. And yet, why not my own? In America, people remade themselves all the time. No law stated that I couldn't be among them.

"How come you and Mom don't live together?"

I had an answer prepared, a sort of official release. "We were kids, high school sweethearts, even—she was there for me when I was in Vietnam. I'll never forget that, Dale."

"Yeah."

"But it got so we didn't have a lot in common anymore. That happens to people, Dale. Your mother's a city person."

"*You* live in the city."

"Well, she's a big success now. I'm—"

But I stopped before I said "I'm nobody" to my own son. "It wasn't her fault," I said, finally. "I had a lot of problems. I got mad all the time—"

"I know."

"And bad luck. I had some of that."

"Mom says you were mad because of the war."

"I'm not sure. I think the war may be an excuse for people, sometimes. Anyhow, I'm trying hard now."

"I love you, Dad."

"I love you. Son."

When he flew home I quit one job—peacefully, with notice—and began another, teaching two classes at the local junior college. And I went in to the paper and took the copy editor's test.

I needed work I could have some respect for. Even more, I needed money.

"We had a nice summer," I told Cindy. "He's a good kid."

"He misses you."

"I'm glad somebody does." I saw immediately that I'd set her up, and I hadn't meant to. It was more a statement of fact than an expression of self-pity, since Dale was indeed the only person on the planet who would miss me.

Cindy didn't so much as sigh.

"I'm doing all right," I went on. "Guy hired me for some mowing—guess I know how to drive a tractor."

"This one runs?"

"Yes. And I'm teaching again. Two classes."

"Great!"

"And some things in the paper—well, one thing. I'm doing all right. You seeing anyone?"

I had been gone from Missouri almost a year, and we'd been divorced nearly two years. Funny how you keep on being married after you're divorced, whether or not you want to be. But I had no hopes of going back to her; the prospect filled me with horror. I wanted a new life, even if it was mean and solitary forever. And, I confess, I wanted off the hook for my failure as a husband.

"Yes, Patrick." Her voice was firm. "I am."

"Excellent," I said.

4

The Hero

THEY GAVE Norman Sims a Silver Star.

There was a company formation with a stack of rifles and helmets before us, to symbolize the men who had died. We stood in the merciless sun for more than an hour, waiting for the Colonel, because there couldn't be a ceremony without him. It began to seem like a scene out of *The Bridge on the River Kwai*.

Captain Keel, whose job was to introduce the Colonel if ever he arrived, gave a rambling pep talk, full of admonishments about drug abuse and social diseases, that I kept tuning in and out of. Mad dogs and Englishmen, I thought, and wondered if I'd passed out. No, I was standing, sweat pouring down my cheeks, and Keel's mouth kept moving in the shrieking brightness.

He respected us. He *honored* us. "Work hard for me, men, and I'll work hard for you," he said, just a working man himself, sick of what was going on back home. He'd come to help. He didn't claim to know everything but by God, if you had a problem, his door was open.

He stumbled away against the white sky, drunk in the noonday sun, I realized. His talk was alcohol talk. "Ten-hut," he managed, as the Colonel drew near, but he forgot even to salute.

Colonel Drake put us at parade rest. He read the citation describing Norman's bravery, and pinned on the Silver Star. He praised the Lieutenant's bravery as well. Not that Sherry had been particularly brave, but he was dead. Drake shook Sims's hand and saluted him, and Sims, who had been endlessly coached on proper behavior by First Sergeant Hickman, tossed off a snappy rifle salute.

Hickman also gave a talk, but his words were drowned out as a Chinook took off behind us, depositing a new layer of red grime on our feverish skins.

Sergeant Ransom received a Bronze Star, though he wasn't at the ceremony. Perhaps the medal comforts him in his old age, down there in Louisiana. Does he still sing the blues? He went to Cam Ranh Bay and lay on the beach for a time, recuperating, before rejoining us in the swamp by the South China Sea.

C. C. Rider was there, but had already reenlisted, and would be gone in two days. He had, in exchange for the next six years of his life, negotiated a nice bonus and thirty days in Bangkok. "They got some great dope in Bangkok," he explained.

I doubt if anyone said anything about his performance under fire, but, of course, that was why he reenlisted. For a week he came around to each of us, apologizing, saying he'd have been a dead man if he'd tried to reach the gun. True, but Sims had reached it, and Sims wasn't dead.

C. C. Rider was the subtle cause of Lieutenant Sherry's death.

More precisely: if he had died reaching the gun, Sherry might not have. Dead heroes. Live cowards. It meant something, finally.

Many years later I was in Amherst, and looked him up in the phone book: Cecil Clarence Rider. He was the only army buddy I ever tried to find, and then it was because I was in town.

I reached his wife. It took awhile to explain who I was, and the whole thing began to seem crazy.

"Just a minute," she said. "I know he'll want to talk to you."

After a long time she returned to the phone and said she'd been mistaken, he'd gone to work, she didn't know when he'd be back.

"What's he do?" I asked.

There was another long silence. "He's doing fine," she said.

They gave me a Purple Heart, merely a medal signifying that you were wounded, more a matter of incompetence than heroism. I kept it for a long time. It's a large, handsome medal which I do not disdain, but over the years I forgot that I had it. I'd run across it in the bottom of my socks drawer and think of ribbons from the county fair, of giant cucumbers and jars of superior pears.

I lost it somehow when I was divorced and the property was divided, though I can't imagine that Cindy would have wanted it.

Sims hadn't been wounded, but he was too shaken to return to the field. As a hero, he quickly proved inadequate.

"I'm a hero, Irish."

"Yes, you are, Norman."

He scowled at the horizon. "With the jaw of an ass have I slain a thousand men!" he declared.

"Calm down," I said.

"Like mighty Samson! Norman the Great, hip and thigh with a monstrous slaughter!" He held up his fists, ran forward like a superhero from the comics, and cried "Zoom!"

But then he followed me, pleading. "What's a hero, Irish?"

"I don't know."

"What's a hero *do?*"

"I don't know. Tries to be a hero again, I guess."

He nodded sagaciously. When new men arrived he took them aside and described in infinite detail his triumphant moment. "I could see what was happening. I knew we were done for! We were fucking goners, man! They had us by the fucking *balls!*" He'd stop with "balls," to assay his effect. The new soldier was terrified.

"They were shooting all up and down the river. Nobody could see where they were but me, I saw. They were running at me and I was mowing 'em down, *banzai!* There were one hundred and two of them. They just kept coming, they weren't afraid of anything, but I shot them all, I got on the gun because C.C. Rider was *scared*."

By now that new soldier was surely skeptical. He knew that one man, Silver Star or not, hadn't killed one hundred and two North Vietnamese. He began to suspect that Sims wasn't a hero at all, when, in fact, what he had done was the stuff, not of Silver Stars, but of Medals of Honor. Alvin York and Audie Murphy— why not Norman Sims?

The new man didn't know if he should be sympathetic to Sims or if he was some joke perpetrated upon every initiate. Sims heard the change of tone in the new man's voice: first, a tremor of doubt, and then an indulgence that was close to ridicule.

So Sims offered his finale. He pulled out the medal itself, greasy by now from handling, and he told about the foot. "Detroit threw the grenade and this boot come back at me? Still laced up. It came off so clean, it didn't even bleed. I was firing and firing and Sergeant Ransom told me to stop and I looked at that foot and then it started to bleed."

Sometimes, Sims cried when he told this part. He didn't mention our dead lieutenant, never cried for Sherry, but somehow that foot had moved him.

And then Sims stopped telling the story. It might even have been that he didn't remember it. I'd see him on the road to the Filipino compound, talking angrily to himself. He'd point toward the village and winding road beyond, and pantomime a sweep with his imaginary machine gun, like Sergeant Rock of DC Comics.

Sims was ever reliable at morning formation, showing up clean and shaven, his uniform straight, his field gear strapped. But he couldn't go to the field. No telling what hell he'd have drawn us into. His babbling nightmares kept him in the rear.

He drew greenline guard several nights, which was mostly a job of avoiding the duty officer, but he had to be removed when he opened up with the M-60 machine gun on a gray, bobbing plane of rats. It wasn't that he was hallucinating, as you might have suspected of the greenline crew. Sims never used drugs or drank. He had simply decided it would be interesting to shoot at the rats.

Some of his rounds went wild and detonated a barrel of fougasse. Lights came on and sirens shrilled and Colonel Drake himself came to see. "Who's that dumbshit set off the gas?" the Colonel asked, and was informed it was the dumbshit to whom the Colonel had awarded a Silver Star.

Drake wanted to send him to the field, but quickly learned, from talking to Hickman and Keel, that Sims was still unfit for combat. They might have cut his orders for stateside at that point, but it offended the Colonel's notions of military propriety to send home someone who so travestied the Silver Star. What an embarrassment Sims would be, even in Warner, Oklahoma.

Perhaps, if the army kept him for a while longer, Sims would calm down and become a killer again.

But it wouldn't do for him to burn shit. You couldn't tell a man with a Silver Star to burn shit.

"Make him permanent KP," Colonel Drake said.

And so once again Sims strutted among those kitchen women, declaiming on heroism, the enemy, manhood, and war—or I suppose he did. Before it all played out I was in the field again. But as I was myself recuperating, I'd see him waving his arms wildly and running about, lifting one boot high like a Thai boxer, crying out like some demented Special Forces bozo in a training film.

The old women and Cuc Hoa clapped their hands and giggled and murmured in a high, appreciative whine. "Dinky dow," they said. "Dinky dow." Translation: crazy. Sims had made a sanctuary for himself, a strangely joyous place under the parachute, amid the bustle and dust and stink of the base itself. I saw him holding up Cuc Hoa's hair and stroking it, and turning her around by the shoulders to lecture her. Soon she was combing her hair behind her ears and pinning it with a barrette.

Sims bought her a dress at the PX. She wore makeup.

Because he was a hero, recuperating from a glorious but officially unrecognizable wound to his soul, and because, too, he made other soldiers so nervous, Sims could come and go almost as he pleased. He saw Cuc Hoa behind the kitchen as she worked, and when he went to Sông Trì Village.

Ostensibly, he went to the steam bath to get laid, a privilege granted only to rear action NCOs who had behaved well.

Field troops could relieve themselves.

Officers were superior to the need.

The steam bath was once a Michelin plantation house, though after the French were routed it had become a regimental headquarters for the VC. Rumor had it that they patronized the steam bath, still.

If so, they must have followed a different schedule than those leonine American NCOs. I was there once in my malingering days, commandeered for a detail to give away captured rice, and went in with the first sergeant from Bravo, a good old boy if ever there was one. There was a sitting room of sorts, done in purple and red, with a desk, paintings of delicate Vietnamese women, and a bamboo chaise longue. There was a plastic Buddha in a pool, sitting squat as a frog below trickling water. Madame Cocoa, a dark, crisp-seeming Cambodian woman, sat reading a Chinese romance through narrow bifocals. She smiled contemptuously and hit a buzzer.

A gaggle of teenagers, dressed uniformly in blue muslin, swarmed about us, pecking at our shirts and belts and undoing our boots, and then we sat sweating out our poisons in the sulphurous steam. Pretty soon, the first sergeant rose, pissed on the rocks, and waddled out for a rubdown from a ninety-pound, fourteen-year-old, flat-chested female. To the girl it must have looked like some big hog was approaching her, but business was business, and for five dollars she'd jack him off. What a life, I thought, not only for the girl, but for the old sergeant, too.

Sims had a different errand, of course. On Saturday nights and through Sunday he stayed with Cuc Hoa and her mother. They lived in a one-room hut behind the steam bath, at the end of what in Missouri would have been called a feedlot. The hut must have been a kind of utility shed back when the steam bath was a plantation house.

The French had killed Cuc Hoa's father, a farmer, an enemy. Her mother was old and weak, though sometimes she stumbled out to the road where soldiers passed, to sell pornographic playing cards, Seiko watches, and souvenir Buddhas out of a suitcase. But she slept most of the time, on a mat near the PX television that Sims bought them. The mother and Cuc Hoa's favorite program was *Gunsmoke.*

In the evenings Sims and Cuc Hoa walked through the village, slowly in the heat. But bursts of energy would overcome him and he'd prance ahead, turn and walk backwards until she drew near again. He'd run away, zooming like a superhero, saving humankind. Cuc Hoa's face would shine with pride and something like a mother's indulgence.

Once, when I had returned to the field, I saw them on bicycles far down the road, almost in Indian Country. She wore her PX dress and he was very much out of uniform in a *nôn la*—one of those conical hats. I waved at Sims but I doubt if anyone else in the truck recognized him.

Still, it was too unmilitary to last. Sims was a different sort of untouchable now. Maybe he could have stood naked at noonday and no one would have noticed, but he couldn't kiss a Vietnamese scullery maid, and play elaborate games and give every impression of having a good time, and get away with it forever.

A lieutenant in Bravo Company saw Sims in the tiny open-air cafe where the boom-boom girls took their tea. That lieutenant, named Dranow but universally thought of as Drano, would turn out to be a kind of nemesis for Sims.

Dranow informed First Sergeant Hickman of Sims's antics. The spirit of it was that Dranow knew Sims was a fine soldier, a hero, certainly, but also a primitive soul in need of guidance. Dranow wasn't malicious so much as career-minded. He meant to cause some trouble, but he also meant to look out for the welfare of an enlisted man, and protect Vietnamese nationals, and win the war.

Hickman dutifully summoned Norman and told him the village was off limits, but by now he had a long and informed acquaintance with Sims and was inclined to look the other way. So the spirit of *his* remarks was: this shavetail is complaining, keep your head low.

It wasn't enough for Dranow. Captain Keel was in the field, and with Sherry dead we had no executive officer, so Dranow complained to the Colonel. In writing. Maybe the army even has a form for it: Foreign Nationals, Fraternization With During Hostilities, Enlisted.

If you went by the book, Sims could have spent time in the stockade. Technically, he was AWOL when he was in the village, and, since Cuc Hoa's father had been Viet Minh, the case might have been made that Cuc Hoa was a VC. And, therefore, that Sims was a VC sympathizer—about to pass along the formula for a new kind of rocket fuel, no doubt.

Colonel Drake was not so simple as that. Besides, he objected to the way Dranow had sidestepped Captain Keel. He thought that Dranow was deliberately trying to make Charley Company look bad, and Bravo Company, his platoon, in particular, look good. He thought Dranow, like every other lieutenant hell-bent on making grade, was lobbying for a job in Saigon once his field rotation was done. Shuffling secrets for MACV: that was the *real* Drano. Eating up men from a distance.

Drake, too, was inclined to let Sims off with a lecture. He was a hero, after all, even if he was a trifle eccentric. Sad to say, even as the Colonel adopted his expansive, almost fatherly mood, Sims informed him that he wanted to marry Cuc Hoa.

"You wanta marry a *gook?*"

"I love her," Sims said.

If the truth were told, she wasn't much to look at. She was big, for one thing, not at all like those demure, diminutive creatures French officers had prized. When such matters arose in this war, it was always in the rear, where the war was remote enough that romance was possible. Even then, to stand a chance for approval, the woman could not be mere kitchen help. She was a clerk or telephone operator, say, a woman who spoke good English. An official approval was slow in coming, and might never come. But here? In a battle zone? With a dishwasher?

"It's a *gook* woman, troop."

"She's nice to me. Back home, I didn't have a girlfriend. She'd be happy there, sir. She likes TV and stuff."

"Christ Alfuckingmighty," Drake said. "Sims, no more trips to the village. I think—"

"Yessir?"

The colonel scribbled something on a pad. "You should see the chaplain."

I stood above the company area at ten in the morning, rubbing my arm recently free from the sling, already exhausted in the heat, my new fatigues stained with sweat and grit. I looked down upon the mess hall and Sims's parachute, studying the shadows that moved beneath.

Something snapped. Their little playhouse infuriated me, and I raced down the hill as if to chastise Sims, berate him for being a hero, *kill* him so there would be space on earth for better men, for dead men, for Lieutenant Sherry.

I stopped short. Sims and Cuc Hoa were seated primly, having tea. On the makeshift table was a pan of peeled potatoes and carrots, a half-chopped cabbage.

Cuc Hoa saw me and nodded, acknowledging she knew me though we'd never spoken. Sims gestured wildly. My anger fled as swiftly as it had come and I felt sad. I understood that, like Sims, I needed a place to rest. Watching those two, I thought that what a man seeks in a woman is not sex but condolence, a spot of tenderness, shelter.

He tries to find his mother.

"Irish!"

I stared at Cuc Hoa, almost an American girl in her PX dress, almost the girl in the trailer next door.

"You haven't met my friend, Irish." Sims came around the table and took her hand. Cuc Hoa flushed. Behind us, the crones looked up once in unison, then dropped their heads and croaked to each other amiably.

"How's that arm, Irish?"

"I go back out next week."

Cuc Hoa made a flowing gesture with her hands. "Great killer."

I was startled. "No, I—"

She said it again: "You look like killer."

Sims jumped up and down. "See, Cowkie? I told you he'd come. I talk about you all the time, Irish. You want some tea?"

I sat on an ammunition crate and Cuc Hoa slid a plate before me, with orange slices and cookies. She poured tea and looked at me anxiously. "You like?"

"Sure," I said, though it was absurd to drink the steaming tea in the middle of the steaming day. "Thanks a lot."

"We have ice," Sims said. "If you want *iced* tea. But this is like, it's like a *ceremony*." He stared gravely. "Aw. Aw. You're sad. You sad because of Sherry?"

"What did he die for, Norman?"

Sims nodded. "Yeah. He was a good guy."

"We have TV!" Cuc Hoa announced. She plucked at my sleeve. "Just like America, we have TV. *Bo-nan-za!*"

I tried to concentrate on her, tried to see what Sims saw. "You live ... with your mother."

"Very sick."

"I'm sorry."

"We live in bad place, number ten." She giggled. "Sometime, pig—"

"We were sleeping," Sims said. "And this pig runs in right in the middle of the night. Cuc Hoa was really mad, she beat the thing in the head with a shoe. It *squealed?* and ran in the corner, only finally it went outside again. We had the door open because it was so hot."

Cuc Hoa smiled dreamily. "We marry," she said.

"You mean you—"

"Not yet," Sims said quickly. "She means we're *going* to be married. They make you fill out all these papers. Irish ... everybody likes you. You got influence! And I was wondering if you'd talk to the chaplain for me."

"He doesn't have any authority."

"You have to go *through* him, and if he says it's wrong, if he says—"

"The guy's a vulture. And I don't have any—*influence.*
Jesus, Sims, you're the one with influence, if you, if you just—"

His chin went up. "It's okay. I can do it."

"He wouldn't listen to me, Sims. Honestly."

"It's okay!"

Cuc Hoa grabbed the pan of vegetables. She glanced at me
accusingly. "Killer," she said.

She was confused. How could she know of my days as a soldier in the peace movement, or that I'd almost gone to Canada?
Yes, in Vietnamese there were always multiple meanings. It
depended on your inflection.

"Cowkie! Irish is a really nice guy."

As I backed away she subdued a look of panic, throwing me
one last, mute appeal. It was clear she thought Warner, Oklahoma,
was a place where you didn't have to sleep with pigs.

I bought a hamburger and Coke at the snack bar, and sat on a
green bench with pad and pen, determined to write to Cindy.

Behind me was the greenline, concertina wire, and the village, in a long slope with a dirt road in the middle, winding
toward the mountains. I was headed for those mountains, where
men who wanted to kill me lived.

How could I write to Cindy, when I couldn't even remember
her face?

I missed Sherry. It didn't seem that he was dead. If Sherry
was dead, there was no goodness left, no gentleness in the world.
I could have been in Canada, but instead I was a captive of war.

I slurped bitter Nescafe as the rain began. It swept over the
shanties and the temple, the rice paddies and rubber plantation. A
group of Vietnamese men who had been laying drainage tile
ducked under an awning made of the tin cans that instant grapefruit juice was packed in. Below them, in the center of the village,
I could see the steam bath. Cattle and water buffalo milled by Cuc
Hoa's hut. Sims, you damn fool, I thought. She's had a dozen
before you.

The rain refused to stop. My letter to Cindy filled up with Lieutenant Sherry, and I threw it away to write to Sherry's mother, but couldn't manage a word. I tried writing my father but he'd never once replied, and every line I had for him was full of hatred.

I tried again to write Sherry's mother, saying simply how much I'd liked him, how all the men had liked him. I figured anything I said was better than nothing. Sherry was dead. Long live Sherry.

What was that silly poster the Doughnut Dollies tacked up down at the club? *Today is the first day of the rest of your life.*

In one hundred and seventy rest-of-my-lives, I'd be home.

All right. Get on Hickman's typewriter and inquire about going back to school. What about a correspondence course? I'd work on my degree right here.

I saw her. My imaginary woman.

She'd been here all along. I must have stopped at this snack bar twenty times. I must have looked at her. Touched her hand.

For an imaginary woman she had an earthbound, profoundly American job. She pulled back her long hair and slapped two hamburgers together, wrapped them in wax paper, slid them through an aperture with a greasy box of fries. It was like she was a prisoner, sliding out her tray.

A tall black kid with his hair cut short sat to eat, his bony legs angling up from the low bench. He smiled warily. Just over from the States, I thought.

The woman's every gesture was subtle and precise, as though she held a slight disdain for her work or it would always remain foreign to her. From behind the screen, in the dark air of a world filled with rain, she remained imaginary. I kept blinking to fill in her image.

Lucky to have the job, no doubt. Flesh and blood, however, like Cuc Hoa. And not as tall as I'd thought.

It struck me that she was staring at me, also. I smiled and she didn't drop her gaze, but neither did she return my smile. I licked shut my envelopes emphatically, went to stand at the entrance.

The rain ended Sông Trì's dust storms and before long the monsoon would begin. The air smelled fresh. It's going to be wet every night, I thought. I need a better poncho.

I turned. There was something from my childhood … words, hanging on in the silence that dwelled above the sound of the rain, in that snack bar ten thousand miles from Missouri: *"Tout de suite, maman. Un moment, un moment!"*

I will, Mom. In a minute! I'd heard French, not Vietnamese or English, and in an instant I knew a thousand things: here were a girl and her mother, holding up their heads by cooking for the American soldiers, ordinary people as in Mountain Vale or Tulsa or St. Petersburg, but coming out of God knew what kind of heartbreak. I spun about. The black kid jumped.

"Parlez-vous français?"

She unlatched a hook and threw open the aperture. She cocked her head sideways and smiled. *"Oui, monsieur. Et vous?"*

"Un peu, trés peu," I told her, that college textbook, the one I'd paid so little attention to, popping to mind. With an elaborate sigh, I added, *"No, Mademoiselle."*

She smiled. *"Quel dommage!"*

"I—*je*—I don't—*Je regret!*"

She laughed merrily. Unconsciously, I had stepped to the counter, and the girl and I bent near in the poor light. Her skin seemed so soft, and I loved how her large eyes darted about. She wasn't beaten down, or sullen, or distant, or fawning. Oh, what I would have told her! Already we shared something, some yearning.

Her mother's voice rose in reproval.

"Le soldat à envie de parler français," the girl called out. She looked at me seriously, and shrugged. I understood that, all right. What can we do about these old folks?

"Il voudrai nous faire mal," her mother said.

"Oh, no," I said. "No bad—no harm. Please—*s'il vous plait*—no harm."

"Ne lui parles pas!" her mother said.

"Oh, maman. Il est gentil. Il est beau!"

"Il est bavard. Un laideron, le soldat Americain! Non! Ton frère, il voudrai—"

The girl sighed. *"Oui, maman."*

"Please," I said. "I really mean no harm. My friend died. *Mon ami?* Please, I just—"

She looked at me mournfully, but began closing the aperture. "Oh, no, no. Miss! Please—"

"Monsieur," said my imaginary woman. *"Bonsoir, monsieur."*

5

Imagining Paradise

I WAS STANDING in the hall, conferring with a dentist's daughter concerning the unfairness of her C-minus, when Jacqueline first clacked by, wearing sandals that strapped around her ankles. I kept staring at those sandals and the red toenails that poked out of them. When I looked up, she was smiling. Your archetypal blonde temptress.

"Hey," the dentist's daughter said. "Hey."

I was filling in at the junior college, hoping the newspaper would give me a call. I was trying to feed myself. I wasn't thinking of love, except at night, sometimes, and all through the day.

Jacqueline was the French teacher. She wasn't a Florida native, but a Bostonian who had fled a worn-out marriage to a moody surgeon. Her husky voice would rise an octave and seem wistful when she described him, as if, having loved the man, she could never truly love another. Even so, when her son turned eighteen and left for college, she felt the marriage was done. *Fait accompli.*

She appealed for my support over a Coke in the school cafeteria. "Once I left him, I found myself."

It seemed rude to point out that I'd heard this story before. My own story was pretty familiar, too: aging divorced guy tries to find his way in a new town. In fact, I had yet to emerge from my

Great Period of Solitude, and for company had no one but the little band of ne'er-do-well veterans, every second Sunday. Wombat was married, but the rest of us had gone so long without women that we should have declared the state deliberate. We could have written a book telling the world why, in celibacy, we were so doggone happy.

Jacqueline owned her house. She drove a sleek white BMW. Her tan was perfect, her teeth sound as her bank account, and she frequented a fashionable spa. She played racquetball. She swam. She went sailing with a physician in Sarasota—"Just friends," she assured me.

For six weeks or so we met for lunch on Treasure Island and St. Petersburg Beach, in those little sandwich shops that cater to tourists and well-heeled widows. It was winter, cool along the beach, and we walked holding hands. Sometimes, we walked in the neighborhoods, and I'd leap up to grab two juice oranges where a tree grew over the walk. But Jacqueline always refused hers, as though picking the fruit, and offering it, was something only a rube would do.

Nothing I did had any effect on her, but I was intoxicated. I lay in bed at night thinking of her perfect body, what joy she would give me, what joy would be hers when at last she understood how tender I could be, how passionate. We'd be a man and woman in Paradise.

I bought Jacqueline flowers and candy, bracelets and earrings, but she hardly acknowledged them. I wrote her letters that came as close to poetry as this hillbilly ever had. I looked into her unfathomable eyes and praised her extraordinary beauty, not just her physical beauty but her exquisite, poetic soul.

She cocked her head impatiently, stared off, and said, "It's an act."

And yet if it was an act, what was it for, if not to attract fools such as me? Had she made the judgment I was someone who mattered, because I occasionally wrote for the newspaper? Did that explain her act? Should *I* offer up a performance, as well? Was it merely a question of the style I so dismally lacked?

Experimenting, I said, "I love you."

"I love you, too," she said, and slid one leg along mine, under the quaint round table.

After lunch and yet another walk we'd sit in her white car and kiss, and part at last in delirium, and she'd refuse to have dinner. I asked her a dozen times, to dinner, to a play or concert, and even to go scuba diving, but always she said no.

"Lunch?" I'd ask again, pitifully.

"Of *course,*" she'd say, and brush her slender fingers, her long and perfect nails, down my cheek.

And other than for lunch Jacqueline went out with me only once, to the Salvador Dali Masquerade Ball, at the Hilton on Tampa Bay. It was one of St. Petersburg's few grand events.

Even then Jacqueline delayed giving me an answer for more than a week. Waiting, I grew furious with her, and swore off women forever, not that there were, or have been, many to swear off of.

Then, as I sat grading papers in the school cafeteria, I looked up to see her in a yellow sundress. "My God, you're beautiful."

She turned her head to deflect the compliment. "May I still go with you to the ball?"

"Sure! I—"

"Can I meet you there?"

"Why can't I come to your house? What's wrong with me? I've done everything, I've been patient, I—"

"We'll have a late dinner, and you ..." She lowered her eyes and her voice. "You can have what you want so much."

Wombat was a docent at the Dali museum, and a fast talker besides, finagling tickets to the ball on the promise that his group would "pull security." Near as I could tell, "security" amounted to standing at the door, not knowing what to do. Worse, the pieces of uniforms we proudly wore soon became costumes.

"Did Dali paint homeless people?" I heard some woman murmur.

Since the homeless flock to St. Petersburg, and so many of them are veterans, we either were parodying the homeless, or ourselves.

At that we were no more out of place than the lawyers and developers, pretending for one night of the year to be wild. Two people made one costume, of a severed head on a table, and there were clowns and fops and court fools, and Little Bo Peep, and characters with garish, twisted faces, after Dali's paintings.

A man in an expensive blue suit sat as quickly as possible at one of the five-hundred-dollar tables, and glowered at his wife, and got quickly drunk. When all the guests had entered, and as the band played and the fancy folk danced, we veterans retreated to a dim corner, and followed his example.

Otto Sanchez had come, not for the ball so much as to be with us a last time. Shortly, he was returning to the VA hospital in Seminole. He had been living with his parents, who were moderately prosperous and had bought him a van, with hand controls and an elaborate system for unloading a wheelchair. But his mother, who had insisted he live at home, died, and his father wanted to remarry. The new wife wanted no part of caring for a middle-aged, handicapped stepson. On top of that Sanchez's kidneys seemed to be deteriorating.

"Come live with us," Wombat said, when the band stopped playing between sets. He glanced once at Katie, his wife, who smiled unconvincingly. "We could fix up that shed out back, get you some cable TV in there—all ground-level. Not too shabby for a crippled guy. You could paint, and—"

Sanchez slid back in his wheelchair, and grinned. "Thanks, man. I *want* to go back."

The band returned and we fell silent, watching the beautiful people dance, thinking of Sanchez. Except that he'd stepped on a mine, I never heard the full story of what happened to him in Vietnam, but to all of us he was a hero.

What Jacqueline did was a small thing, and cost her nothing, I suppose. She took it upon herself to cheer us up.

She laughed merrily at the weariest of jokes. She asked in detail about Wombat's job, a decent carpenter's job but hardly as fascinating as she pretended. She sat beside plump Katie to discuss how the women in the crowd were dressed. It made Katie, who was out of place here and felt uncomfortable, relax. Soon both women were laughing at the pretentiousness of it all.

Jacqueline was radiance itself, and when I rose to take my turn again at pulling security I looked back at her and marveled. Several men asked her to dance, and her eyes fluttered across the room at me, as she gracefully declined. She knew the importance of solidarity among the troops, of making it seem as if she were mine. What a fine wife-for-a-night, I thought, and knew every man was envious.

I also knew that I hadn't a prayer. I was too obvious for her, and too desperate.

I don't think Sanchez even glanced at her. Women were a painful subject with him. But Jacqueline kept looking at him, and, finally, came around the table to put an arm on his. He tensed. She bent near his face, and said, "Won't you dance with me?"

"No, no."

There was an awkward silence, as if we all were wondering if she were trying to hurt our delicate hero. She threw back her head and laughed. "Dance with me, soldier!"

Sanchez reddened, and edged his chair backwards. She shook her hair, and said almost wistfully, "Please? Such a *handsome* man!"

He nodded. Jacqueline stepped behind his chair and rolled him to the floor, which was crowded but gave way to the Anglo and the Latino, the racquetball player and the paraplegic. The older, uncostumed couples had come forward as the band slipped into its obligatory slow number, "Quiet Nights under Quiet Stars."

They danced. Jacqueline took a step forward and Sanchez, his head lowered, rolled the wheelchair back on one side, slid away with the other, in time with her. They made a slow circle around the floor, under the whirling lights. Sanchez's head went up, and he laughed, and when the music quit all the crowd applauded not the band, but this odd couple.

Jacqueline fetched him a beer, not knowing he was forbidden alcohol, and walked beside him out of the ballroom, down

the thousand carpeted, circuitous paths of the huge hotel. Not
exactly jealous, I followed, spied them at last in a dark lounge.
Jacqueline was nodding emphatically. Sanchez spoke slowly, deliberately, with great conviction. He had a thousand things to say.
Somehow, this night of the ball, he could say them to Jacqueline,
when he had said them to no one else. The secrets of heroism, perhaps, and how to be happy. He spoke in Spanish, and she
answered in Spanish. Her eyes were bright with love.

And it was all phony, an *act* of kindness rather than kindness itself, but Sanchez was fooled, so wasn't it preferable to the
truth? The truth, after all, was that Otto was doomed to a slow
death at the VA hospital.

All that Jacqueline did for Sanchez—leaning down to adjust
his collar, brushing his cheek with a kiss—was, if not quite a lie,
then a sort of audition for the grand role she sought to cast herself
in. Jacqueline went through life auditioning. She wanted romance,
bravery in the face of incalculable risk, and noble sacrifice. Small
wonder I never came near her heart. It was not that I was a rube,
but that I was an *ordinary* rube.

After the ball I followed her home. No late dinner, no soft
talk: she met me at the door, and led me to her bedroom. She
peeled off her dress and her underwear and lay on the bed, arms
crossed demurely over her breasts, one long thigh lifted slightly.
Her tan skin gleamed.

I fucked her almost vengefully and she clawed at me and
later, as we lay beside each other, I saw that her blonde hair had
brown roots and that the wrinkles around her eyes, once her
makeup had run, were as deep as my own. Over and over, men
seduce themselves, as women know they will.

In the morning, as I kissed her good-bye and asked her to
dinner on the following evening, she averted her eyes, then bravely
lifted her chin to announce that she had taken another lover.
Rather, I was the other lover she had taken, and now the old one
liked her better because I had found her desirable as his attention
was beginning to wander.

C'est la guerre.

We'd had all those lunches on the beach, I realized at last, because she was unlikely to be seen there. We made love because, in her mind, it was a way of ending things, rather than beginning them.

I guess she was no damn good, but for a few glorious moments she seemed like the meaning of life. For Sanchez as well, and maybe neither of us had a right to more, and were fortunate men. Still, why are there no wives like the one she auditioned for? Why is it that the thing you want most turns out to be mere fantasy?

6

By the South China Sea

THE JUNGLE BROKE open and there was the South China Sea. It was warm and dirty, like some ancient, fecund place where life is born, and where it rots. It was at my feet, and it seemed I might walk upon it: it could not be wetter than the leech-infested earth.

I stood watching for a pretty bird or a boat or any sign whatever that life went on somewhere, that my dim memories of childhood and learning and love were not outright delusions. There was a breeze and I felt a moment of peace. I rolled out my poncho liner and lay in the sun, dazed, sweat stinging my little wounds.

The gunners set up positions in a semicircle facing the jungle, while the rest of us dropped our gear and gingerly peeled off our clothing, as if it were skin or skin would come with it. On the muddy shore we washed ourselves, revealing flesh that was disconcertingly vulnerable, as brown, black, and white men alike cleaned sores and burned away leeches.

Worm had a Frisbee, and threw it at Dietrich, who threw it to Jim Cole, who threw it back to Worm. Worm dove, sprawled, and lay still for a moment. I imagined dying with a Frisbee in my hand, lying there while some North Vietnamese pawed over me. What would he make of it? Little man with a big rifle: *"Cái này là cái gì?"*

Jim Cole drew seawater in a canteen cup and splashed it across Detroit's thick chest. Detroit ran after him, lunging in and out of the water, until Jim Cole skidded on the slimy submerged surface and fell. Detroit twisted Jim Cole's arm behind his back. It looked strange, the huge black man, naked, genitals bulging, grinning above the Indian. Buffalo soldiers and red Indians, good as any to fight Communists.

"Don't, man," Jim Cole said. "Please, don't."

"Shee-ut," Detroit said, in mock outrage, and waded toward a sandbar, massive and inevitable as a bulldozer.

Jim Cole repaired to the shore, where he turned a backflip and walked on his hands ten feet or so, as if his minor acrobatics could cancel Detroit's minor offense.

Ransom sat on his helmet at the edge of the water, soaking his feet. There were open sores circling his back and abdomen, all from the days since he was shot. He turned now and again to eye the jungle. He watched Jim Cole and Detroit, and I tried to read his face, but I could never tell what he was thinking, or if he was thinking anything.

Once, back at the base in Sông Trì, I woke in the small hours from a treacherous dream of some unidentifiable blonde, woke in a sweat. And there were a hulking big man and an agile small one, Detroit and Jim Cole, creeping out. To smoke a joint, perhaps, under the tropical moon. As I turned on the bunk, settling to sleep again, there was Ransom, watching.

We went so long without women they became mythology. An actress, Yvette Mimieux or Ann-Margret, became part of your memory, real as the girl next door. Yet if we sat naked on a sandbar in the South China Sea it was because nakedness, like skin color, had ceased to matter.

It no longer occurred to us how it might look to Mom and Dad: this company of scabbed, unkempt men barely removed from animals, naked beside each other, laughing and grab-assing by the yellowish sea, where brontosauruses might have raised their heads from the weeds, and pterodactyls swept low.

As we swam and sunned ourselves the helicopters began flying in our resupply, fanning far over the calm water and into the sun, then pouncing upon us, struts clawing into the sand. The first lift was clothing, and Detroit surfaced from the deep water, sea-weeds draping from his shoulders, and waded back ponderously, to find something big enough to fit. Jim Cole threw him trousers and socks and shirts, and the two were buddies once again.

The mail landed, the beer and soda and rations, and for half an hour there was fierce trading: three packs of Pall Malls for one of Winstons, one can of C-ration apricots for two of fruit cocktail, four Upper Tens for a Black Label.

The chaplain landed, chewing on a short cigar. He had a talent for arriving when you had reached your weakest point. He'd pray with you. And he would never bring up reenlistment directly, only in the course of his counseling.

Two replacements arrived, and a South Vietnamese scout named Tru Vu. Many years later, I learned that there was a well-known poet named Tru Vu, and in fact our scout, who was anything but well known, wrote poetry, too. He wrote it for his wife, who lived in Hue. He slid off the helicopter with a broad grin, revealing one gold tooth, a receding chin, and the merest curling stubble where a goatee might one day grow.

He tried to look fierce, carrying his rifle with elaborate casu-alness, as we did. He was barely five feet tall and all the clumsy American gear seemed too much for him, but if the North Viet-namese could tie two-hundred-pound bags of rice on their bicycles and ride down miles of narrow paths, maybe this little man was durable enough. We would never quite catch his name and so he became "True Blue."

Everyone noticed True Blue immediately but pretended not to. We knew how ARVNs were. You called for artillery from one of their bases only as a last resort: they might lob every round into the sea, or wipe you out with white phosphorus. One time a com-pany of them was to link with us at a hot landing zone, and when they came in they clung to the helicopter struts. The door gunners stepped on their hands to put them into fire.

True Blue turned round and round, grinning. Finally, Captain Keel saw him, and waved impatiently. Battalion had sent True Blue because, supposedly, he knew the mountains, where we were bound if the swamp ever ended. In concert with Bravo Company, we were looking for a regiment of Vietcong.

The first replacement was a Puerto Rican named Luis Bareiro, whom, shortly, we christened Screwy Louie. He'd offended his company commander in Alaska by smoking too much dope and going AWOL. Attempts to freeze him to death failed, and, one day at morning formation, he was handed his orders for the sunny South. He'd been in the rear for several weeks, claiming fevers and chills, but he'd run out of excuses.

He looked over our camp and, mournfully, out to sea. He dropped his gear and sat on some C-ration boxes, chain-smoking, with a towel hooding out under his helmet, making him look a little like a Legionnaire. He patted his chest as if about to heave up something. He drank from his canteen, grimacing as he swallowed. His hair was sopping already and his face dripped sweat.

The other replacement was Norman Sims. Silver Star Sims.

"Why they send him?" asked Dietrich. "That fucking *goose.*"

"He save your ass, dude," Detroit allowed.

Norman saw me, smiled, and came sloshing his way across the miserable earth. An Okie by the South China Sea, lost. Lost the more in saving us.

"Hiya, Irish!"

An hour of daylight remained when we moved into the swamp again. Two separate cargo flights had drawn fire out there, and a PsyOps group had monitored some radio transmissions that didn't connect with anything. Deduction: lots of Vietcong, all mixed up with NVA regulars.

Captain Keel gathered the platoon leaders and showed them where we had to go, though it all looked the same in the swamp. Slowly, the men put their gear together, wrapping letters and cigarettes three times in plastic, and placing cans of fruit to the outside, where they'd ride against canteens and stay cool. I walked over to help Sims but he was fine.

Ten meters into the green of palm fronds and tall grass, the yellow water was gone from sight. Men staggered with their full packs, caught their balance, pawed the ground, and snorted like horses.

Our second squad had the point and drove slowly inland, almost painfully in the heat. Captain Keel tore the horn from his radioman's hands and screamed we'd be humping until midnight unless the point got moving. Tough guy, I thought. He'd get a lot of us killed.

Then again, maybe not: the heat was so intense it dulled the senses. Keel had to inject menace into what was merely routine simply to make us move. "They been jacking off all day, get the lead out!"

"Yes, suh," Ransom said. "I pass that on."

"You damn well do better than pass it on, *Platoon Leader,* or I will personally ream every ass in your command."

"Yes, suh. I pass that on."

Ransom himself went forward, but he had only a few weeks left in-country, and to allow him to point was criminal. Second squad rallied, pushing through the brittle elephant grass in bursts of five meters. One man dove out to flatten the grass with his body. Two others sliced with machetes, until all the file had zigzagged from the sea, and we were buried in green.

The air bled moisture. With every move I broke into a sweat, had to pause, daub my eyes with a towel, guzzle my precious clean water. For an instant I propped the barrel of my rifle under the brace of my rucksack, to lift the weight off my back, before stumbling breathlessly on. Sweat ran down my belly, down my thighs inside my trousers, into my socks.

You could feel light-headed, falsely energetic, and if you didn't swallow salt, and drink, you'd stroke out. In your faintness a prickly vine would catch your towel, and you'd jerk back and the vine would rip open a trail along your arm, and blood would glisten mixing with sweat. And you'd fall.

Ransom had spared Screwy Louie from the point because of his newness, but now, with every man spent, threw this last resource against the heat. Louis chopped for a time and broke through onto higher, more open ground. I dropped where I was, panting, and stared as the rest of the company drew by and formed a circle. I slurped down a can of peaches.

The Captain dropped his gear in the center by a tall pine, incongruous among the mangroves and stands of bamboo. The air was as stifling as an attic; I took shallow breaths and shuffled forward, trying to find a spot where the stench of methane didn't sear through my head.

True Blue followed, grinning. He didn't appear tired in the least. He built a small fire with heat tabs and squatted to eat scorched, round chunks of C-ration ham.

"Boocoo VC here," Keel said hopefully, pointing to the map.

"Oh yes," True Blue said, nodding eagerly. "Boocoo VC."

As darkness fell Ransom and I crawled out of the hole we'd dug, a shallow, muddy affair in the root-bound earth. We stretched ponchos for our hooch and to catch water in the holy event of rain. In another day, if it failed to rain, we'd drink the sour swamp.

In the starless night there were three quick explosions and a brief roar of machine gun fire. Bravo Company, sweeping the swamp parallel to us, had sprung its ambush. Word came they had killed three VC, but, best of all, they had no wounded, were not themselves pinned down in deadly trouble. We would not have to scoop up our gear in the dark and stumble to their aid.

Some big animal splashed. I lay slowly down and kept going down, tunneling into sleep. Dietrich and Worm argued over bug juice, and I meant to tell them to shut up because they interfered with my dreaming, but I'd lost the ability to speak. So I could only think it, *shut up, shut up, there aren't any mosquitoes here,* and then Ransom shook me awake for guard.

Sims had grown plump after his weeks of KP. Through the next day's march he looked at me steadily, as though I were one of his tormentors, but he didn't speak. Once, I touched his skin, and it

was trembling and hot, like an excited dog's. If he had had the
point that day he wouldn't have made it.

"You okay?" I asked, and waited for him to speak, but he
merely nodded and set his feet to follow mine. When again the file
stopped, and again Keel screamed into the horn, and again
Ransom went forward to help, Sims dropped in his steps and
stared off blearily. He was a hero, but had little experience in the
bush, or with the brute boredom of the swamp.

Yet in a week he was as filthy and lean as any of us. He was
quiet, helpful; he did his job. Sometimes, as we waited in ambush,
he withdrew, but he no longer talked about saving the day or the
severed foot. Instead, their doctrinal differences put aside at last,
he and Worm talked of a personal relationship with Jesus.

"I tell you what it says in Scripture, Worm," Sims would
offer, and Worm would reply, gently, gravely, "Oh, Norman, I
pray for our captain. Every morning I pray for him."

It was as if my mother had joined the platoon. I remembered
her tireless, agonized pleadings for my disbelieving soul.

Once at night Jim Cole shook Sims awake because he was
talking in his sleep. "They shouldn't have sent you here, my friend.
I thought they would send you to the World."

"No," said Sims, sitting up. "Oh, no."

Sims had been *banished* to the swamp, stripped of every
privilege, exiled. If he lived, he filled a slot. If he died, maybe it
validated his Silver Star, but either way he was no longer a
problem. What harm might he do in our criminal company? He
wouldn't be opening fire on battalions of rats or running off to the
village. He wouldn't be falling in love with gook women, taking
up the time of colonels and chaplains.

Sims could have sought counseling. Better, he could have
written his congressman, but the matter never went beyond the
chaplain.

What difference could I, merely a squad leader, have made?
I could not have spoken with any enthusiasm for Sims's cause,
Miss Cuc Hoa. And if Sims, a hero, had no authority, what "influ-
ence" could I bring? Later, I thought that if only Sherry had been

alive, it might have amused him to make Sims's argument, but Ransom and I were only enlisted men. Down deep, we also thought Cuc Hoa was just another gook, who might be shooting at us two weeks hence.

The chaplain's argument was religious, and while Sims wasn't convinced, he was stymied. And the more articulate his protest, the more the Colonel concluded that here was a man recovered from battle fatigue, altogether fit for the swamp.

Sims's table and chairs were taken away, down came his outrageous parachute, and again the mess hall looked as it should: grim and sunbaked, scrubbed clean.

Worst of all, Cuc Hoa lost her job. One day she was there; next day, she wasn't.

Did our chaplain offer a cold Pepsi? Did he clasp his soft, freckled hands, and listen sympathetically? Was his method to appear to be on Sims's side? "It's wonderful to have the opportunity to visit with you, Norman. To share with you a few of my thoughts. Everyone is very proud of what you did out there."

"Yessir."

"What we forget sometimes is that the Silver Star is not only a great honor, but a responsibility. You're an example, Norman, someone the men look up to."

"I am?"

"When we are far from home—well, I know *I* get a little lonely sometimes, don't you? But we can never forget that we are guests here. Are you a Christian, Norman?"

"Yessir. Yes, I am, Chaplain. I took the Lord Jesus as my personal savior when I was—well, that was when my daddy left, and we moved to Warner. I guess I was—"

"Faith?"

"What? Oh, you mean denomi*na*tion. We're Freewill Baptists."

"And so you believe in the Bible."

"Yes, Chaplain."

"Let me read something to you. Deuteronomy, Chapter Seven. 'Thou shalt smite them,' that's the enemy, Norman, and you *did* smite them, 'and utterly destroy them,' you did that."

Sims slapped his fist into his palm. "Like mighty Samson!"

The chaplain blinked. "Yes. 'Thou shalt make no covenant with them, nor shew mercy unto them: Neither shalt thou make marriages with them.' You understand, you understand what's being said here? *No marriages with them.* It's no reflection on this Vietnamese girl, but when we're a long way from home, it's easy to forget, sometimes. In Nehemiah we read—"

"You mean Cuc Hoa," Norman said. "You mean the army don't want us to get together."

"We read that 'They clave to their brethren,' that's the Jews, Norman, God's chosen people, 'to observe and do all the commandments …'"

"You're saying we shouldn't mix the races."

The chaplain fingered his collar. "The *Bible* says it, young soldier."

"It says that in the Old Testament, but how about the Good Samaritan? He's from a foreign country, and he turns out to be a good guy."

"That's not a matter of race. I'm not saying, we're not saying, that any particular race is—"

"We shouldn't be Good Samaritans to people of other races?"

"Of course I don't mean that! Norman—"

"Didn't Jesus say that the many shall come from the east and the west?"

The chaplain sighed. "He didn't say to get married, Norman. Think about this girl for a moment. Think about the trouble she'd have in Warner, Oklahoma."

"Nobody would care."

"Your church. Your mother."

"Nobody cares what we do."

"Have you ever thought—how bad these people want out? What a good deal for your little dishwasher! Ever thought of that?"

"Did you ever love anybody, sir?"

"An American woman! Not, not an Oriental."

"She's just a *person*."

"She's a God damned *dink* and I want this thing ended, Mister, right here, right now!"

The earth tilted and we wandered in a plain of bamboo. It had not been bombed and was virgin, mammoth. Clumps of it had trunks eight and ten inches in diameter, a slick wet green that rose branchless for twenty feet and sealed off the sky. The ground was even, with a deep layer of packed dry leaves. In the mornings red worms came up out of them, and squirmed like little snakes.

Keel split the company into its three platoons, and we leapfrogged one another on our slow march to the mountains. He'd grown hoarse from screaming at us, but relented once we were beneath the bamboo, not marching us far in a day in this cooler, darker place. There was time to play casino and chess, write letters, dream. Louie managed to get high every day.

Keel called me over in the long twilights, offered me Player cigarettes, a beer. For some reason he liked me, or liked who he thought I was: a confidant in his past named Jones. I had given up on teaching him my name.

"What about this Jane Fonda, Jonesy?" he asked, holding up a *Newsweek*.

"Liked her in *Barbarella*, sir."

He giggled. Several beers, I thought. Something more than beer. "Showed her little titties, didn't she?"

"Yessir. Fine little titties they were, sir."

Sometimes, we came upon evidence of battle: a litter of C-ration cardboard, a circle of foxholes, or a bunker complex that had served for a hospital. There were broken cots, mildewed bandages, decayed riggings for traction. The bamboo was splintered and brown here, and deer browsed between the craters. The sky poked through.

Keel insisted on examining every shell casing and hooch pole. He strode off inside the perimeter with Ransom or me in tow, nodding, expostulating; he whirled and pointed; he kneeled, tracing the leaves with troop movements and strategies. He'd get on the radio to discuss "developments" with his lieutenants.

We'd make an early camp and send out patrols, which, not at all in character for commanders, Keel led himself, even taking the point, sometimes.

We found smoldering campfires, bloody earth, and bloody shirts that could only have come from contact with Bravo, since we had inflicted no wounds. We stepped across wide red trails with a hundred sandal imprints. One night we saw a mysterious green light far out in the woods. Keel sent a patrol, but they found nothing.

We heard laughter ahead on the trail, and we all dropped and waited; I could hear the insects buzzing, the cranes calling. But the talking ceased and no one blundered into our guns. We all knew that VC base was there. We could sense it like trouble down a dark street, but where was it?

We slogged through a bayou, the bamboo a latticework above. Here and there the water was deep and I was afraid of it, of plunging under and never coming up. Though Keel forbade it because it announced our position, sometimes the point men opened up on cobras. I'd follow and see goo splattered along a limb.

But it was Sims who spotted the python. It was thick as a flagpole and twelve feet long, draped over the crotches of three clumps of bamboo, splotched brown and green like the bamboo itself. It was sluggish. Keel came forward and stared for the longest time, but he hadn't a word. There was no point in bothering the thing, but abruptly, in his idea of impressing Keel or in some lunacy peculiar to heroes, Sims leaped forward with a machete and hacked behind the snake's head. "Fuck you, fuck you, fuck you!" he screamed, shocking Worm and me if no one else, as if the born-again Christian were possessed of demons, or the python had the head of a chaplain.

The python lashed about, busting up bamboo. Louie and Dietrich leaped in with their own machetes, but the snake was tough, mostly cartilage, and moving, besides, so that it took several minutes to sever its head. It writhed to the ground and went on thrashing. Sims and Louie and Dietrich looked up in bloody triumph, but Keel stumbled back, a grin plastered over nausea. I recalled him back at Sông Trì, reeling in the noonday sun.

Now the bamboo closed in. We had maps, every hour we calculated coordinates, but we were lost. Your eyes couldn't penetrate the green for more than a hundred feet, and what you did see was clump after clump of bamboo, each clump identical. The branches arched above to form a tunnel burrowing away in a dozen directions, sealing off the sky, and it was as if we trudged through catacombs. Late in the day, rain fell on the mat above as onto a roof, thunderously. It dripped through, down my back, into my eyes. A boil rose from my neck, and I rubbed it and rubbed it again, but it grew until I felt lopsided.

The men trudged like the gray figures of a dream, seldom speaking and then only in whispers, their duties so deeply routine they went about them like zombies. The night swallowed us up. There might have been deer and monkeys, birds or bats or buffalo, but you couldn't hear them for the bamboo. No other sound like bamboo: creaking, chafing and moaning, shrieking with the rise of wind. Perhaps, through the branches, you spied a sliver of moon, and in the eerie light fancied you heard men talking, zombies, too, arguing in Vietnamese. I woke and the wind had ceased and the animals gone silent. I tried to think of Trudy or Cindy, but they were too far away, like radio signals you can't quite hear. And it began again, like some spirit stealing up on you: bamboo. Bamboo creaking.

It was on such a night, twenty days from the South China Sea, when Keel's nightmares began. "Oh," he moaned, and his voice carried as if he were next to me. He shouted: "Granville! Is that you?" I rose, and with Ransom stumbled to his position.

"Suh," Ransom said. "Please, suh. No."

"I'm sorry," the Captain said, like a child who'd wet his bed.

It went on for the next several nights, in the silences before dawn; I'd slip over with Ransom and the medic, and hold Keel by his shoulders. For no reason I understood, he trusted me. "Don't tell anybody about this, Jonesy," he said. Sometimes, he screamed like a wounded man, and I wanted to shoot him full of morphine. "Hush now, suh," Ransom told him, in a hoarse whisper.

"Did I do it again?"

"We has to be quiet, suh."

"A dream. I'm all right now. My uncle, his name was Granville—"

"Granville, sir," I said. "Please be quiet."

"He only had one arm, Jonesy! He used to try to hug me, and it scared me, when I was a kid—"

"In the morning, suh."

What the medic gave him helped, but still, in the daytime, Keel's face was swollen as from a sting, his eyes bloodshot. You could see him laboring to hide a kind of guilt, reaching out to any man who'd look at him in an appeal for understanding, even forgiveness. But the men avoided his eyes.

"He's sick, Irish," Sims said. "Poor guy."

"Let's hope he doesn't get us all killed."

There was nothing in these woods, I said to Keel. Bamboo was like that: full of ghosts. He said he knew it, that he'd lost his confidence briefly, simply lost his bearings. It could happen to anyone. Sometimes, as the sedative overtook him, I wasn't Jonesy but Daniel, his son. Daniel was in college, and a draft resister. How was it, Keel lamented, that a construction boss, a man who had belonged to the union, a man who had served in the Guard for seventeen years, could raise a son who was a draft resister?

We came to the shore of a murky, black lake. As I pulled the last guard, slapping and pinching myself to stay awake, there was a loud crack as of a limb breaking, and a splash. Keel had risen and walked into the lake. It was a miracle he hadn't drawn fire.

"Lights!" he screamed. "Lights! Lights!"

Ransom and I hurried to find him, across the ground glimmering with moonlight. We waded beside him, glowing, and the water, lapping away, was like flowing silver. "Shut up!" Ransom said, when Keel protested.

"Lights," he explained. "Don't you see the lights, Jonesy? Over there, across the lake, in the bamboo there. That's where they are. All this time!"

"It's the moon, sir," I told him.

"We've got to report this. Call in artillery. Sgt. Ransom—"

"It's just the moonlight," I said. "You see things that aren't there. They wouldn't give themselves away like that. You *never* see them, sir. Calm down. Please, sir."

"Don't they ... go in boats?"

"No, sir."

"Oh." He let himself be guided back to his position, where we laid him down and covered him. Sleepwalking, I thought, but it wasn't merely that. It wasn't nightmares, really. It was fear, mixed up with his uncle and the son he couldn't understand. It was his fear, wanting so much to count for something, that he wouldn't.

Ransom whispered violently into the handset. He woke up Colonel Drake.

It was like a conference of Indian tribes: the brutal, fatalistic Bravo; the regretful, weary, dream-plagued Charley. Friends who had not seen each other since basic training stood looking at what they had become, and compared notes on who had been wounded, who was dead. Bravo hadn't found the VC base, either, though twice they had sprung ambushes, killing four men, and six.

John Keel flew out before noon, banking over the steaming lake with hardly a salute to acknowledge him, but free, unless he had been forever silenced, to tell stories to his fellow Guardsmen of his valor under fire.

Anyhow, we were captainless. A soldier in Lonely Platoon shot his foot a few minutes after Colonel Drake flew in, in reaction to the rumor that Drake would be our new leader. It was as if Drake were Ahab and the VC regiment his white whale. What man would sign on to *that* voyage, at least if he'd read the book?

"Did it on purpose," Sims said.

"A lot of people thought *you* did it on purpose, Norman."

"No, I-rish!"

It would have taken a direct order from Creighton Abrams himself for Drake to have assumed command of a line company.

He'd paid his dues, or there was no point in being colonel. He paced the shore, brandishing maps, pointing toward the mountains, while Ransom and the two lieutenants, and the captain and lieutenants from Bravo, shuffled their feet and vied for favor.

Keel's bird had drawn fire going out, and Drake's had drawn it coming in, so the Colonel had a hunch. Call it a vision: of hundreds of little men milling in the jungle, down in a pocket of bamboo between two great rock formations, a river flowing outward toward the black lake. The rifle fire had come from a spit of growth at the apex of the two rock formations, and from the air it seemed suspicious. An observation post, the Colonel was certain.

It must have been written down somewhere from the beginning, and sealed away in a heavenly vault, that until a real captain could be found Lieutenant Dranow would take over our platoon—and the company command as well. No doubt the Colonel understood ambition, since he was afflicted with it himself. He didn't have to like Dranow to make use of him. Maybe he was exactly the man to pinpoint those VC.

If he moved Dranow and his men to join with our platoon, and split off the rest of Charley, the Colonel had three companies—all of them understrength, admittedly. But one company could attack frontally, the other two could come from behind, and the slimy little devils would be done for.

Was there another medal in it for Norman Sims? What else could it mean, when Drake turned and pointed directly toward him? And Dranow's head went up in a wise nod?

Vision revealed, the Colonel was gone in a whirl, and Dranow's men were upon us almost as quickly. Dranow stood in full gear at Sergeant Ransom's position, as Ransom broke down his hooch and tossed his hot chocolate into the lake, keeping his eyes low, saying nothing.

Questions were not in order. I did not understand what was happening but it was urgent, at least in Dranow's mind. I scrambled for my gear. Suddenly, I was running. Were we under attack? Sweat stung my eyes and my pack banged against my kidneys. Down in a sink, I fell to one knee in sluggish water.

"What *is* this shit, man?" Louie said.

"Nothin," one of Dranow's men said. "Just the ell-tee."

We left the bamboo and entered a plain of crumbling lime-stone. Some relative of the banana plant grew from every crack, alongside stunted willows and oranges so twisted and dwarfed they could have been bonsai oranges. I sat in the shadow of a pockmarked boulder, fingering the boil on my neck, panting a little. I would have screamed but I was surrounded by strangers. Still, what if I *had* screamed, screamed and screamed and kept screaming? Wouldn't they have had to do something? Wouldn't they have sent me away?

"I'm going to die," Worm whispered.

"No, you're not," I said, though I wasn't so sure of my own fate. "Pray."

"I can *feel* it, Irish."

Ransom, looking worried, and compromised by his usurped authority, threaded back along the file and knelt beside me.

"That thing gonna bust," he said, pointing at my boil. "We okay here?"

"We okay," I said, for his sake.

Worm squirmed and nodded.

"Private Sims!"

Like the rising moon, a head appeared over Ransom's shoulder. Dranow smiled benevolently, hardly acknowledging Ransom and me. "*Norman.*"

Sims stood. "Yessir."

"Pleasure to meet you, at last." Dranow shook his hand. "The tales we've heard in Bravo Company!"

"All good, suh," Ransom put in.

They'd just as soon kill him, I thought. We must all have thought it. Dietrich, surely the least among Norman's defenders, popped up, danced, threw a mock-punch. "Everybody likes Norman, sir."

Worm was dizzy from the heat, perhaps, and from prayer, so that it sounded like he was talking about Jesus. "He saved us all."

Dranow smiled ironically, shook his head at inexorable fate, and led Norman up a jagged rock. He pointed toward the mountains like some great explorer, and maybe he talked about destiny. He must have been inspirational, because the fierceness, or the madness, that had captured Sims when he slaughtered the python once more glowed in his face. He seemed to grow physically, pulling in great breaths of air even as the Lieutenant pumped him up. Yet, coming down from the rock, he might as well have wagged his tail.

What else could he do? Could he say no? Could he scream it: *No! No!* Screaming had served Captain Keel, in the end, but could you scream deliberately, not from madness but sanity? Maybe, for the sake of discipline, Dranow would grab the medic's .45, and shoot you in the head.

Dranow motioned for us to draw near. He, too, was pumped up, as if it were the Ten Commandments he offered. "This is a combat assault, men. Into a hot LZ." He spoke softly. "This is a charge."

"*Jesuchristo!*" said Louie.

"Shee-ut," said Detroit.

"Delta Company—"

"We *Delta* Company now?" asked Ransom. "No, we Charley!"

"*Delta* Company," Dranow said, looking meaningfully at his second-in-command, "will take out the gun."

"Just a rifle, Lieutenant," drawled a sergeant, one of Dranow's men. "Just one little bitty rifle."

"We don't know what's *behind* that rifle. The Colonel says it's a regiment. Do you know more than the Colonel, Sergeant?"

There was silence. Every officer had learned about assaults in school. One in five harbored a secret desire to try one. But to the enlisted an assault had one universal meaning: dead men.

"I will lead Yankee Team," Dranow said. "Private Norman Sims will lead Alpha Team."

"Will this win the war, sir?" I shouted out, but no one chimed in.

Dranow looked at me contemptuously. "There is no room for doubt in an action like this. You don't think how thirsty you are, how your legs won't work anymore. You don't think of your *girl*friend. If you think, you're afraid, and we have no room for fear. You aim your weapon. You fire. Because you are a machine. A killing machine." Dranow thrust out an arm. "That's why Norman Sims could do what he did."

He meant it, I thought, and I was a little in awe. That was one helluva officers' school down at Benning. Maybe Dranow himself would teach there one day, marking the blackboard with little x's where the bodies had fallen.

"Sims," I said, as we began moving again. "Scream!"

"What?"

"Scream, scream!"

"Calm down, Irish. We got a combat mission!"

"Dammit, Norman, think for yourself!" But he stared at me as if I were a traitor, brushing past and yelling, "Alpha Team, *here!*" We were running again, milling about, grouping frantically, as the helicopters came skimming over the treetops, dropping through our red smoke.

All of us had crawled on and two helicopters were aloft when True Blue stumbled from the brush. The pilot turned, jerked a thumb angrily. Jim Cole, all muscles, reached down to help, and True Blue crawled aboard.

"What we do?" True Blue asked.

Good question. I dangled my feet over the struts and bent my head low. Worm read from the little New Testament he always carried in his shirt pocket. What was that old line—no atheists in foxholes? Once, I stood in a foxhole, and, for a joke, called out, "There is no God!" But at the moment I wanted to be like Worm, because Jesus gave Worm discipline. I remembered what Cindy said, and my mother before her, that only faith could get you through. But I had no faith, and couldn't acquire it simply because I needed to.

I closed my eyes and tried to assess with precision how tired I was, what my body was capable of, as the cold air rushed around me. Stay alive, I thought. Don't let this maniac Dranow kill you.

Ransom studied the passing woodlines. Jim Cole chewed gum furiously, and his legs twitched.

The door gunner passed out iced Cokes from a canister chained beneath his perch. "Going home!" he shouted, and Worm, his face wonderfully calm, said, "Where you from?" but the wind tore away the man's answer.

The birds came around in a line and tipped downward. The door gunner opened a tin of smoked oysters and passed them around to commemorate his leaving. My uneasy stomach turned looking at the oysters: they were oily, viscous as snot. I vomited, and Worm and Jim Cole pulled back from the door in alarm.

I bent my head to my knees, reached to the boil on my neck, squeezed violently. It came into my hands: a clot of yellowish goo and a little dribble of blood. Worm looked at me in horror, clenched his rifle at port arms, turned away from this work of the devil. I saw it in his face again, the knowledge that he was about to die.

I shook my hand and the worst part of me dropped away into the bird's shadow, spun on the clouds below. And I was all right. I could drop into battle not already wounded.

The gunner tossed his Coke to the skies and drew erect. He spoke into his radio and I thought, the pilot knows. There's no one down there, he knows. "Cold?" I shouted. "Is it cold?"

The gunner shook his head. "Hot," his lips said.

Jim Cole thrust up his palms like a traffic cop. "Hot! Hot!"

Hot. Of course, it was hot. Well, okay then. My head was clear. I could do this. I tucked my towel carefully under my pack straps and pulled them tight. I reached to ease the tip of a grenade out of my bandolier.

The gunner fired, aiming down at first, then locking into the woodline. Tracers crackled into the underbrush, and I watched for an answering volley, a wisp of smoke.

Blat blat blat blat went the rotors, as the bird blew flat the grass. There were jagged rocks everywhere. The pilot couldn't land, and we rocked in the air thirty inches up. I bent out, mustering the nerve to jump, measuring my fear of landing badly against the knowledge that I presented a perfect target. Two birds ahead, I saw Sims leap and run almost without faltering, and, in the birds behind us, Dranow's men jumped, rolled, and staggered toward the woodline behind their leader, who had knelt and lobbed off a round with his grenade launcher.

Ransom leaped, and all of us followed. I hit soft ground and rolled, rose to one knee, brought up my rifle. I looked: Worm was alive.

"Alpha Team, move out!" Sims yelled, and ran forward in a crouch, and turned, chin strap buckled, commanding us to follow. He was wide-open, as he had been when he took out the gun by the river. He's a fool, I thought. He's a dead man.

As we struggled to our feet, leapfrogging forward in crouches and crawls and little running bursts, Sims kicked high over bushes like a man leaping hurdles, holding out his rifle and spraying the woods with one arm.

Dranow nodded approvingly. He jumped up like a rabbit and ran to the safety of an overhanging rock, calling in artillery even as he moved, his helpless radioman tripping and falling behind him, so that the cord to the handset was stretched to its length.

Yankee Team, like Alpha, came up slowly, not charging, not assaulting; only Dranow and Sims had fired. At last, as artillery shrieked in and obliterated the woods, both squads grouped. I came last, propping up Jim Cole, who'd twisted an ankle between two rocks as we dropped from the birds.

Otherwise, no one was hurt. And no fire had returned, if evidenced only by the fact that Sims and Dranow were still standing. So we followed the drill this time, dutifully laying fire and moving up as Sims pranced out before Alpha Team, emptying magazines into the menacing trees. Dranow's men laid down fire, too, and moved up in a semblance of order, while Dranow charged like Custer himself.

No one was there, and there was no sign anyone had been since God on the day of Creation. Dranow and Sims turned about for their photo op, and no one openly ridiculed them. We had been too scared, and now we were too weary.

＊　　　＊　　　＊

I was standing by a mortar crater, tipping back a canteen, when Screwy Louie killed the officer.

Quick draw: the enemy came down the trail going south; Louie was going north. Louie let fly a full magazine, nineteen rounds in six seconds. Back in the file I thought, this is it, there are hundreds of them, and I dropped and waited. Sims, no longer the leader of Alpha Team, pressed his face into a tree and his pants leg darkened. Finally, Ransom signaled for us to rise.

Screwy Louie was gasping when we drew near. He squatted, holding the dead man's helmet out before him like some papa-san winnowing rice. He drank water, spat, drew to his feet. "Fuck *this* shit, man," he said.

Dranow shook Louie's hand. "Outstanding," he said. He was pleased the dead man was an officer.

You could tell he was an officer because he wore one of those worthless Russian watches. Karl Marx should have been on the dial, jerking his hands around. Dranow handed the watch to Louie, whose eyes filled with contempt. *"Gracias,"* he said.

But the officer had also carried a sheaf of plans with elaborate drawings of bunkers and fields of fire, and Dranow thought we were close at last to the regimental headquarters. Because of the drawings, two nights later the B-52s made a strike. I could see the arcs the bombs made, like chain lightning, down on the sea.

The bombs didn't kill anything but lions and tigers and bears, oh my, and now that VC headquarters seemed like pure myth, like the elephant burial ground in Tarzan movies. Some thought Colonel Drake and the generals he consorted with had dreamed it up to keep us on edge.

Late one afternoon, as we ascended a high trail alongside a stream, Dietrich shot a big gecko. Birds flew up in a red storm, like music to accompany our startled thoughts. As if in protest the ground itself seemed to tilt, folds of earth heaving up between the slick, wet banks. I clutched at a root, slipping even as Dietrich's rounds echoed, and went rolling through leaves down into a slough, like a child in October in those blue Ozarks hills I still could recall.

I made no cry, for it was as if all the sounds in the world had been used up. I lodged in a bowl of leaves far below, sinking to my chest before my feet touched rock. I stamped at the leaves to make my way again, and looked up. The company had disappeared, on the precipitous, high trail.

I imagined myself a North Vietnamese, small but deadly, in ambush of the gawky Americans. My fall had been quick, silent. What if, as he rounded a bend in the trail and leaves shielded his eyes, the man behind me, Worm or Sims, did not realize I was gone? What if I lost them, and had to find my way alone to Sông Trì Village?

In another instant, this seemed like a woods anywhere, in the Ozarks, perhaps, in Shannon County, every square foot alive with rodents and birds and beetles. I wanted to lie here like Rip Van Winkle and let the leaves fall around me. Take the men away, the Americans, the Vietnamese, and there would be no war. Give this mountain to one side or the other, leaves still would fall.

I heard a groaning and short panting. Sims slid down the slope, eyes leaping about. Further back, coming more cautiously, were Worm and Dietrich, Detroit and Ransom. At last, Sims saw me, gave me his hand, pulled me from the leaves. "We were really worried about you, I-rish, we can't lose you! We couldn't make it without you!"

"Oh." I looked away. I was almost sorry he'd found me. "Yes, you could, Norman."

The monsoon began. It rained ceaselessly for two weeks and the mountainside ran with water. I put my foot down not in soil but in deep green moss over crumbling rock, and water stood in my tracks, in the dents of my trail. Off the rock, great ferns had lifted from the red mud, and there were violet mushrooms large as buckets, and vines in a mat all around, dripping with rain. Countless birds flew, fearlessly, ahead of us and over the ravines far below, hovering before the waterfalls like clouds, red, orange and white against the dazzling green. Over the green rolled a blue mist, clinging to my hair and skin.

My arms, cheeks and legs became wonderfully smooth. But on my neck, where the boil had been, a row of abscesses rose like tiny craters, tender red between them. At last the supply bird brought dry socks, and I took off my boots and saw the gashes between my wrinkled toes. I put on the socks and drew my boots together tightly, alarmed at my body's decay.

I grew obsessed with my rifle, wondering if it would fire. I took it apart and oiled it three times a day. I spilled the slender orange rounds from their magazines and wiped and oiled each one.

Now and then there would be an opening in the canopy, a surprise. I could see down the mountains, see the sun lying on the green swamp and the black lake, shining in the rain that fell in streaks down where the B-52s had hit. Yet farther was the South China Sea from which we had come. Destroyers sat on it now, the merest lines of gray, on gray. It was ten minutes for a helicopter, and five weeks on foot.

Talk had ceased. Sounds, of feet plunging and squishing, or the hoarse whispers of men, or even the distant, bitter firefights of Bravo Company, had so little resonance they seemed like recollections. Worm had diarrhea, and kept drawing off the trail a little and dropping his pants, all while the rain beat down. He returned wan and embarrassed, stared wearily ahead. Sometimes, Sims huddled with him, urging him on in their shared faith. Sometimes, in the heavy rain, they opened their Bibles and found a solacing verse.

But for me Worm was only a curiosity in the soundlessness, not to be sympathized with or laughed at, another blurry episode in a dream. Worm staggered another three hundred meters and retreated once more up the mountain, and as we waited for him Cobras plunged in the rain, their miniguns belching soundlessly, and their rockets drawing lines down the gray sky, coloring the rain like Roman candles.

True Blue walked into an ambush and the two men behind him were killed, and, slowly, I realized one of them was Worm. So he was right. His Lord had spared him only to take him a few days later. Ah, I thought, it's purest chance.

Detroit shouted, "Down! Get down!" but his voice seemed distant, like a radio transmission. Yet we knew what to do, all of us at once, one thought. A mortar exploded in the trees and seemed like no more than a limb cracking in a storm; the smoke was gone instantly. As our machine guns pumped into the moun-tainside, I saw the medic rise. Worm came staggering, his faded green shirt bloody and running with diluted blood, and he fell beside me, dead, and the medic and I wrapped him in a sogging poncho liner and that was bloody, too, and the Medevac took Worm away in the rain.

"Worm was nice!" Sims said, crying.

"Yes," I said.

"He was—he was *sweet.*"

"Yes."

As if Worm's death were a sort of sacrifice, even as the heli-copter bore him off, the rain stopped and the sun emerged. We made camp near a waterfall, in a clean pine woods with a mat of needles beneath. I lay on a flat rock in the sun to let my sores dry, watched deer play on a far, grassy slope, and slowly wrote a letter to Cindy, dozing off and awakening to rain pelting my face, breaking into sweat again in the claustrophobic heat, sweating onto the letter. I wrote about Worm having shit all over his legs, and threw the pages away. I told Cindy about the deer, and speculated that she was a college woman now.

We lay under the pine trees for five days, mustering our strength, trying to connect again with speech, remembering that we couldn't tell a joke or trade a can of apricots to Worm, because Worm was dead. We bathed in the pool beneath the waterfall, glo-rying in the cold, clear riot of water beneath the trees and envelope of heat.

The chaplain flew out to hold a short memorial for the dead men. Afterwards, Sims cornered him, and they parted in anger. The chaplain stood in the open area, pointing, and Sims's head went up defiantly. Dranow watched intently.

He seemed bored with us, or, more precisely, bored with the failed mission. He repaired to a hooch that lay on a flat outcrop-ping of stone above our swimming hole, and steadily ignored us. I sat in the shade, dozing to *Pickwick Papers*. There was a flut-tering as of a great bird, and I looked up in time to see Dranow, arms outstretched in the flight from his high perch. He clipped neatly into the green water, surfacing by a log that had snagged in the rapids downstream.

"Shee-ut!" Detroit said.

"Amazing, Lieutenant!" Sims said.

Dranow combed back his hair with his hands, glanced over us, and smiled slightly. Then he climbed to his rock again, where he surveyed the broken land below and wrote in a spiral pad. His memoirs, no doubt.

Three days later, as we stumbled up the last grade toward the plateau, Lonely Platoon, bringing up the rear, reported movement behind them. It was standard procedure to blow "movement" away, and so they did. I was near Dranow, who grabbed the radio before the firing began, but swallowed back his words.

It was True Blue, who had stopped to smell the flowers or record a beautiful thought. Lonely hadn't deliberately killed him, perhaps, but it was the sort of thing where you'd think, wait, this is wrong. Don't fire. *Dùng ban!*

Once more we wrapped a body in a poncho liner and called for the Medevac.

Dranow walked to the landing zone and studied True Blue's dead face. "Jesus," he said. "The paperwork on these nationals."

We weren't ready for the Medevac. It came in behind us, swooped off high, hovered and delicately turned, a great butterfly. The sun reflected off the rotor blades, made a sort of stroboscope, so that the birds flocking up high seemed to hold still for an instant.

Usually when a body went out no one looked, but this time everyone did. I didn't know him, I thought. He was with us six weeks and I hadn't even said hello to him, asked about his wife, his poetry. I shunned him like everyone else, like the bad luck he proved to be. If I could have traded his life for Worm's, I cheerfully would have, but I couldn't get used to how he'd died.

We killed him.

The ground leveled and the trees became weeds, until we were walking in an abandoned rice paddy. We had reached the high plain where Sông Trì lay, we had climbed the mountains, and wherever we had been, whatever we had done by the South China Sea, it was finished. Dranow studied the horizon, called Battalion, motioned impatiently to Ransom.

Everyone knew what was happening without being told. A new captain had arrived on the base. Having eaten us up, Dranow was headed back to Bravo.

7

Summer in Paradise

I INTERVIEWED for three reporting jobs and for one as a copy editor, but white males, particularly if they were only marginally qualified, were not in demand. I thought that being a veteran might help but, as the editor told me outright, only if I were handicapped. I *am* handicapped, I wanted to say. Every day, I drag my useless self up these steps.

Finally, the paper offered me a job in Proof, and I gave notice at one of my part-time jobs. I held on to my classes at the community college, dashing in as they began and leaving immediately, to avoid Jacqueline. Later, fool that I remained, I began looking for her, and learned that she was on sabbatical in France.

That marked two years in Paradise.

Quickly enough, I understood that Proof wasn't a sexy department. Proof, in fact, might as well have been called Death. You were blamed for mistakes and yet poring over galley after galley looking for them was the dreariest of tasks. The only other member of the department was an old foreign correspondent putting in his final months before retirement. It made him no difference if we misspelled Riyadh or ran "affect" when we meant "effect."

I'd gone from dishwashing to its professional equivalent, but, even so, it was an improvement. The newsroom was air-conditioned, and you could do the work sitting down. In fact, if my colleague was any guide, you could lean back in your swivel chair, and snore.

Not long after I began work a story ran about how, in the tortured heat of late summer, Vietnam vets were reminded of the jungle. The climate in St. Petersburg is nearly the same as that of Saigon. The implication was that Florida veterans were time bombs who could break into violence at the least provocation.

The woman who wrote the story was the same one, Stephanie, who had so admired my own reminiscence.

She was pretty in a severe way, as if being attractive embarrassed her. She was not flirtatious; I doubt if she knew how to be. Her work was her entire life. She had a bead on the *Washington Post* and, not long afterward, that's where she went.

I objected to Stephanie's story. The veterans I'd met in St. Petersburg and Tampa were down on their luck, but they weren't violent. Hadn't veterans had a tough enough time of it, without turning them into crazed killers?

She pulled back from the computer screen. She fingered her glasses nervously and folded her hands. "I'm really sorry for those guys," she said, and looked up at me with her plain, brown eyes. I think that Stephanie was one of those people from whom I learned, finally, the truth of my mother's homily: a soft answer turneth away wrath. Disconcerted, I lowered my head and walked across the newsroom to the little cell where I did my reading.

A week later an air force veteran, an ex-policeman from Virginia, killed two women in Sarasota, one of them his girlfriend. He turned himself in to a veterans hospital a few hours later, claiming he thought he'd been in combat. Stephanie, now the paper's expert on veterans' affairs, wrote the story.

Maybe the two women were lovers. Maybe another man was involved. Maybe the cop's combat flashes were real, and maybe, after the fact, they were a strategy for the courts. It didn't matter much. Even if the guy was calculating enough to establish his insanity, he was still a murderer.

Stephanie began making excuses to come over to my desk. She struck up conversations in the cafeteria, and, dense as I can be,

I thought it was because I was a veteran and she felt sorry for me. One night when I couldn't sleep I started thinking about her, and realized that she, too, was lonely.

Sometimes, though, nothing happens even if you want it to. We had dinner once and two days later I called her, but she was on assignment down in the Everglades. When she returned, whatever moment we'd had was gone. She retreated far behind those glasses and we hardly spoke. I could have pursued her but, at the time, was still obsessed with Jacqueline.

Weeks later, my mind full of commas and misspellings, I glanced across the newsroom and saw Cindy. I rose from my chair.

It was Stephanie, of course, who, from a certain angle, looked like Cindy when she was twenty-five.

I sat outside a laundromat on a Monday afternoon in August, on one of St. Petersburg's famous green benches. When you are alone a long time you have thoughts such as, how many people have sat here? How many old folks, how many Okies, how many grieving wives? It was cooler on the bench than inside, near those gasping machines, and I slumped with my eyes half-closed. Stephanie was wrong. Nobody could be violent in such heat.

Three TransAms roared up with their loads of Vietnamese. This and half the laundromats in town were their territory. TransAms, Firebirds, Camaros—James Dean lived on among punk Vietnamese.

I thought of the "cowboys" in Saigon and Vung Tau, who rode in gangs on Honda motor scooters bought from the profits of pimping and black marketeering. These Floridians wore black shirts like the cowboys, and hats, but I couldn't recall that the original cowboys had possessed those fancy tennis shoes.

One young man jerked his eyes toward me as if suddenly recognizing something, and I was startled. His nose had the same sharp angle of a dead North Vietnamese from long ago, on Firebase Sheila, the very day I joined Charley Company.

The young man smiled, and I nodded in reply, but thought of that dead soldier, smiling, too. I closed my eyes for an instant, remembering. It was one of those almost academic puzzles that plague you through life: how you can smile as life seeps out of you.

The dead man was part of a human wave attack, faceless, numberless men who snorted opium and charged machine guns. Maybe the opium made the soldier smile even as he stared down into the gaping red hole that had been his stomach.

A man who's been dead for three days, frying in the sun, is mostly methane, and we couldn't go near the bodies without donning gas masks. The bodies crumbled when I touched them, revealing maggots and poisoned water beneath. I couldn't understand what I saw, couldn't believe it, as if the bodies were props for a horror movie, as if my life had become a series of special effects.

Ransom and I loaded the bodies onto trucks and drove them to a great pit by the South China Sea. There we dumped them and covered them with lime. The smiling soldier stared up at me, though as an abstraction now, a vague detail amid the wreckage of bodies.

In another day, two days, the bodies had cooked until they were one friable, liquefying mass of water and ammonia and dirty lime. Finally, the dead man's smile was only a swirl of grease in the hot wind.

I opened my eyes. I never dreamed of those bodies, even of the smiling one. They were a horrid memory, but not a nightmare. Thank you, Stephanie, but I was not about to break into violent rage.

Still, in some sense the pit of dead was always with me, even as the local boys jumped about, flexing their muscles and kicking out with tae kwan do moves.

The St. Petersburg smiler shrugged to make it clear there was no menace about him, and I offered a two-fingered salute. It was as though we meant each other well but had no idea how to communicate. He jumped in his car.

This new generation of cowboys seemed trapped by the laundromat, going around it again and again, as if the great world beyond their circle were too puzzling to enter. Where would they be in thirty years, as my generation tottered toward the grave?

Would they, too, be veterans? Would their own sons, knowing not a word of Vietnamese and no more of ancient cultures than I did, go to fight in Asia again, or the Mideast, or Africa?

They bought Cokes and returned to their TransAms, laughing, dancing. They drove away, their stereos thumping fearsomely, like drums.

There was a large Vietnamese population in St. Petersburg. Many were middle-aged women who had raised these punks by themselves because their husbands lay dead in Vietnam. They seldom found new men. They worked in the city's kitchens, or they were maids, or they packed fish.

Their daughters were quicker to adapt than their sons. They were keen on education, careers, fine houses.

It was the story of immigrants. Like my veteran friends who had become artists, the Vietnamese were a result. Event had followed event and it meant nothing in particular, as my own sorrow meant nothing.

Snap your fingers, I told myself, and sorrow is joy.

8

The Village

WE LAY WITHIN an island of trees, pines and bamboo, enough green to hide in. Eventually, we would walk into Sông Trì. For now, Bravo, harder hit than we, was guarding the base, sending out their patrols into the rubber plantation, building up to strength.

Our latest new captain was a crisp, no-nonsense soul brother named Bell, who flew out once to break the company into squads again, then flew back to Sông Trì. The squads made camp around the abandoned rice paddy, three kilometers apart, to observe the enemy's movement. There wasn't any movement and the days were long and sunny, the nights cool. We grew lazy and odd.

We were closed in on three sides by a desolate woods. The old paddy sloped to working rice fields, the rubber plantation, the road and, finally, perhaps ten kilometers distant, the village. It was soundless within the little woods except for the wind and the occasional squawk of the radio, and we would go five days without mail or any contact with the rest of the company. Our weapons seemed like camping tools. We were Boy Scouts. This was Florida.

There was still no letter from Cindy. She was a conservative young woman, and I assumed I had offended her with my talk of Sims's thwarted nuptials and deer grazing on the bloody hill.

But there was a package, wrapped in brown shopping bags and addressed to us all. Inside was a big round tin holding a cake, and it had made its journey, in truck and jet and C-130 and helicopter, intact. I placed it on a tree stump as a sort of offering. It was hard to accept the cake, to comprehend it, to recall the world of its origin. Dietrich put his thumb in it and gouged out a piece, and I wanted to slug him for marring such a beautiful thing. And yet that's what the cake was for: eating.

It was from Mary, but who was Mary? Then someone saw the return address, Ephraim, Utah, and we realized the cake had come from Worm's wife. None of us wanted it then, or to read her letter telling how much Worm had "loved us." Loved us? *Us?*

As one man, we backed away, and it was long after dark when we approached the cake again, and wolfed it down, because it wouldn't do to have it there in the morning. All those letters, I thought, and still he was dead.

A stream ran from the woods and into three bomb craters, each lower than the last, each filled with scummy, foul-smelling water. A rusted Renault truck lay partly sunken in mud alongside the stream, and, as the days passed, it occurred to me this might have been the last action here: Viet Minh ambushing the truck. Or, perhaps, the Renault had been some farmer's produce wagon, and bombs had destroyed it.

Dietrich dammed the spring with logs and rocks and sandbags, as he had a creek in South Dakota on his uncle's farm. It took him ten days and he wanted no help; possibly, it was the crowning achievement of his young life. He had an entrenching tool but worked mostly with his bayonet, patiently slicing through trees like some demented beaver. He sopped about shirtless, his boots untied, dragging logs and huge rocks.

When he had finished, he seemed a little disappointed that his labors could not be still more Herculean, and paced the woods like a prisoner. He picked a fight when he saw Sims reading the Bible. "You believe in God, Norman?"

Sims didn't talk much anymore. He looked like he didn't want to answer, that it was only with an effort he could understand the question. "Yes."

"Worm believed in God. What good did Jesus do him?"

"Oh," moaned Sims.

"What kind of God would make a war? Does it say in there?"

"Hey, babes," Detroit said, rising.

Dietrich grabbed the Bible from Sims's hands. "Does it say? Is it in red letters?"

"Give that back!" Sims said, reaching, but Dietrich held the Bible away. Sims beat at his chest.

"You little shit. You wanta fight? All right, Mr. *Alpha Team,* I'll fight you."

"Lay off," I said, stepping between them. "Let him alone."

Detroit grasped Dietrich's arms from behind. "Give the man his book. Man wanta read the Bible, he allowed to."

"This is sweet time, Dietrich," I said. "Settle down!"

Dietrich yanked away. He threw the Bible into the water and Sims plunged after, rescuing it without much harm, patting it frantically on a towel. He waded to the other side, and regarded us in horror.

"It's okay, Norman," I said.

"It don't mean nothing, Norman," said Screwy Louie, his longest speech in days. "Mr. Dietrich, he dinky dow."

"I'm sick of it," Dietrich muttered. "People so sorry for him, fucking twerp."

His ankle healed, Jim Cole came in with the resupply, carrying dope. Dietrich stayed stoned most of the time then, a red-eyed, nearly naked swami, long hair tied back with a green handkerchief. Still, he prowled with his rifle, never asleep. I'd see him in the moonlight crouching above his dam, eating the B-2 units of crackers and cheese, on guard.

The woods had a high population of lizards, chameleons and big Tokay geckos, called "fuck you" lizards because they woke you in the morning with their cheerful, gurgling "*Uck-oo!*"

"Fuck *you,* asshole," Dietrich said, and was about to open up, when I tore the gun from him.

"Hey, dude," Detroit said, looking slowly up toward the lizard, and nodding.

"Oh, no, man," Screwy Louie said. "You give away our position in the woods. I will help."

Louie shinnied up trees and waited for hours, sometimes, until the lizard emerged, concluding, if lizards conclude anything, that this was his usual pristine world. Then Louie would grab him around the throat.

Meanwhile, Dietrich whittled sticks with his bayonet and fitted them closely into an elaborate cage. Shortly, he and Louie had a menagerie.

They'd get high and stare at the lizards, but it was disappointing. The lizards didn't *do* anything, except, after a while, kill each other, or die from boredom. Dietrich was for letting them go but Louie had an idea. Together, they cleared a runway. Holding it down, Louie soaked his lizard in lighter fluid and struck a match. It streaked down the runway like a fizzing firecracker, and stopped abruptly, very dead.

We grouped to either side of the runway and placed our bets, which of two flaming lizards would streak further. We did that for three days until there weren't any more lizards, but by then Jim Cole's contact had sent bottles of liquid opium to mix with the marijuana, making such powerful dope that even Dietrich was becalmed.

Detroit and Jim Cole would get stoned first thing in the morning and spend the day together. There was an aura about them, so that it was hard to think of them as separate; the fierce and the methodical, the gentle and the quick, all melded in the sunshine. They cleaned Detroit's gun, laying out the parts on a poncho liner like a jigsaw puzzle. A checkers board came with resupply. They made pawns of malaria pills, rooks and queens and knights of bottle caps or corks, and played interminable chess.

"Shee-ut," Detroit would say, when he was checkmated. His voice was like the sound of bumblebees, ambling over a garden, sonorous, doleful. "I come home one evenin, an there my daddy in the '49. I figure he go for feed. He shift, then he see me an slow down, then he step on it. Blacktop too hot on my feets, I run home in the woods. It so dry. Red dust on everthing. Mama, she come out in the yard. Screen door close: *bam!* They was a bluejay up in the chinaberry tree, I was watchin that ole bluejay, an she grab me. 'That nigger ain't no father a yours,' she say. 'We goin to Detroit, hon, you an me.'"

They swam behind Dietrich's dam, speaking in murmurs that never quite resolved into conversation. Jim Cole dove and disappeared for a full minute, it seemed, and Detroit growled low, like some befuddled monster, until Jim Cole went through his legs beneath the water, and he lifted the smaller man up. They crawled onto the bank and lay naked in the sun, motionless and obscene, like fat snakes.

Once in the starlight I woke to see Detroit on top of Jim Cole, and I stared at them without moving, as curious as I was shocked. I blinked, seemed not to see them at all, and rolled over, staring at the moon's long reflection on Dietrich's little pool.

I enrolled in an English literature course that ended before Dickens, going through it as fast as the mail would allow because, if we went searching for ghosts in the swamp again, I didn't want to carry the huge textbook. I wrote essays and sent them to the University of Minnesota, taking elaborate care that they were dry and unsmudged, proud that I was reaching out for a measure of beauty in this land of dope and burning lizards. I wrote two pages on Wordsworth's line, "Getting and spending we lay waste our powers," which I thought profound though not terribly relevant at the moment. In fifteen days my essay returned, marked "100 Excellent" in a rounded hand.

Nothing could have meant more. I thought of Lieutenant Sherry, and it was as if I was carrying a torch for him. I wrote a long, passionate essay on the lonely perfection of daffodils. In fifteen days it returned, marked "100 Excellent" with the same rounded hand.

Nice, but it seemed to me that the person with the rounded hand ought to appreciate the extraordinary effort I was making, and offer real comment. I wrote a somewhat less enthusiastic essay on Shelley, and enclosed the postscript, "As I take this course I am waiting in ambush for the North Vietnamese. I appreciate the high grades, but who are you?"

In fifteen days my essay returned, marked in a rounded hand, "100 Excellent."

Who could be so insensitive? Some graduate student, perhaps, active in the peace movement? Some old fellow, going through the motions in what was for him a thankless, rote task? Yes, he had had a heart attack, and was in semiretirement; I shouldn't expect much from the old goat.

Or maybe it was a stern, objective *expert,* whose few words went for a premium. He understood my genius and wished to encourage me, but knew that too much encouragement, offered too quickly, would destroy me. All the world was implied in his, or her, "100 Excellent."

On the other hand, maybe no one was reading my essays at all. Maybe the rounded hand was a rubber stamp. I wrote a nice paragraph on Byron, but proceeded to describe the burned-out Renault, Dietrich's dam, and the gecko races. I closed with, "God bless us, every one!"

In fifteen days my essay returned, marked "100 Excellent" in a rounded hand. There were also a letter from Cindy and the papers for my promotion to sergeant.

I threw the textbook into the creek.

Suddenly, Sims began crying.

It was embarrassing and, at first, I tried to ignore it. It was infuriating. We'd been given safe duty, almost fifty days had passed without a shot being fired, and our hero was too stupid, or self-absorbed, to appreciate it. I was sorry for him, but I was more sorry for Cuc Hoa.

It grew worse. Look at Sims oddly and he'd seem to collapse, to await your accusation, to beg your forgiveness. The crying went on for a day or so, and I almost got used to it, like Jim Cole and Detroit's sunbathing. We were all playing poker when Dietrich jumped up and shouted, "Stop it!"

Sims drew a sharp breath and ceased crying. In moments, he was bawling, almost screaming. Dietrich picked up his rifle and headed for Sims with the butt end. And yet this was nearly routine: Dietrich simply wanted to force the issue. Detroit grabbed his rifle, I stepped in front of him, and, muttering, he turned away.

"What's wrong?" I asked Sims.

"You guys won't ever let me play. You guys don't *like* me. You guys—"

"Well, if you hang out by yourself all the time, and act weird—"

"You make fun of me. Dietrich—"

"We don't make fun of somebody with a Silver Star. We're alive because of you, Norman."

He looked at me in horror. He plopped his head against the trunk of a tree and didn't speak. But after a while, nodding to himself, he came over and sat with us. Dietrich, God bless us every one, dealt him in.

It was silent poker. We all were stoned, and the game went on until someone murmured a change, from draw to stud. A game of Guts, where we held cards to our foreheads and bet on what we couldn't see, made us roll in laughter. We played all day, sometimes, passing joints, pausing for a swim or to urinate, in silence under the hooch. We had been paid twice here in the woods and there were heaps of funny money, piasters and military payment certificates. Who cared about money?

Sims won. I had been prepared to teach him the rules, and he won two hands in three. Soon he held all the money and somehow, though I knew it couldn't be, it seemed like he'd hustled us. "Hey, I got it all! Look at this money," he said, holding it under Detroit's nose. "I'm really good at poker."

"Don't *mean* nothing." Detroit lay back with a towel over his eyes.

Sims grabbed the money and walked around the hooch twice. He leaned low again. "You guys want it back?"

No one spoke.

"I don't need it, you want it back?"

"No, man, you *win* it," Screwy Louie said.

Sims took the money and piled it inside the hooch. "There. You guys take it." He walked to the dam and stood looking back. No one grabbed for the money, though in a moment they would have. Some time had to pass for the matter to become casual. The money didn't mean much but, still, there was nearly two thousand dollars in the pile, and it made the game real.

Sims hurried back from the dam, grinning widely. "I know. I'll give it to Cuc Hoa."

"Shit, man," Jim Cole said.

"That gook bitch?" Dietrich asked. "He means that little—"

"Easy," I said. "He won the money."

Down in the swamp, things slithered over you in the night: spiders, scorpions, gigantic centipedes, bold rats. Sometimes, I couldn't sleep because of my fear of them, and sometimes, even long afterward when Cindy and I were married, I dreamed of them slithering over me, once screaming aloud. Night creatures, scurrying about in the blackness, were more frightening to me than those little men with a cause.

But it was different by the paddy. There were no crawling things—no lizards, certainly—and the solitude, so rare a thing in the army, was splendid. As the men snored I stalked the woods, stopping where they grew fearsomely dark, and a foul wind blew up out of that hellish swamp; and I slipped down to the Renault truck and sat behind the wheel, in moonlight bright enough to read by; and I lay beside Dietrich's pool, looking at the stars, trying to spot the Southern Cross.

I thought of my father. By Dietrich's pool I lay writhing in near physical pain, reliving the time when Dad came charging into my room, angry that I'd bought a Chubby Checker record. Why such a silly memory, given all that were possible? Maybe that was the moment I left him behind, and the two of us declared ourselves at war.

"Damn nigger bebop," he said.

"My money! My money!" I screamed, and threw the glass of tea I'd carried from the supper table into his face. I was bigger than he. I could *hurt* him, as he used to hurt me with his belt when I'd done nothing. Nothing, at least, but sass him. Wet with the tea, he shook his head and turned wordlessly away. Suddenly, he was a thousand years old.

I thought of my mother, a woman emboldened only on the subject of religion but to whom, as I entered adolescence, I still could talk. "I want to be great," I'd say to her, as we sat under the maples, snapping beans. "I want to be the best there is at—at *something.*"

"You can be," she said, and seemed to believe that I could.

"Didn't you ever want to be ... the best?"

"To be the best person I could. To be a *good* person, Jimmy."

What came next was, in my eyes, a kind of betrayal: she'd witness to me, saying that I should put my fate in the hands of the Lord. Faith would get me through, rather than talent or ambition or hard work. Rather than the star-crossed destiny of a born genius.

When she was dying, and Dad and I sat at the foot of her bed, she commissioned our pastor to corner me about my unsaved soul, and I thought, *This is so unfair.* Under such pressure, even the old man swore he loved Jesus, because where was the harm? In lying to your mother in her final hours? "I will, Mom. I'll live a godly life," I blurted at last, and saw triumphant love in her eyes, before hanging my head in shame. Oh, why are there no sons like the one I pretended to be?

In the deep quiet before dawn I'd think of girls, chronicling them from the first grade forward, willing myself from misery to tragicomedy. What was her name? I stuffed crayons up my nose to impress her, and was sent to the nurse. Eventually, she was consigned to the slow reading group, the Cowpokes, while I soared into Top Hands. Not comprehending her fallen status, she crept up behind me on the playground and kissed my neck. I socked her in the stomach and was sent to the woman principal, who explained that you didn't hit girls, not in the stomach, at least, because it might prevent their having babies.

There were the girls I'd had crushes on but was too shy to approach, and a girl on the school bus whose honor I defended even though she didn't want it defended. And there was Cindy, whom I planned loyally to think of last, but somehow Trudy always replaced her, like a problem that can't be solved.

I'd imagine sex with Trudy, remembering the peculiar way her eyes glistened in the darkness, her unknowable, animal expression. There was a gravity and earnestness in her eyes, as if sex were a political statement.

Girls banished the last of the night's terrors, until the trees came. They rose like the soldiers I was guarding, gray and greenish-gray and green: the eucalyptus, the rubber, the pine, friends who had disappeared and returned. Weakened from artillery fire, one of them cracked in two at last, snapped in a blinding streak of sunlight.

At last, the birds: one peppy and irregular, like the first rush of steam in my mother's pressure cooker, another that sounded like a killdeer, and a third that screamed like a jet.

The insects shrilled, reached a high pitch, and stopped. All the east had turned orange.

Bones aching from sitting on the damp ground, I stepped to the dam and dipped water into my canteen cup. I propped the cup over my lucky tin can stove, the one I'd carried for six months, and lit a heat tab. I stood on the shore again, sighed lovingly, and leaped for the center. I hit bottom with an oozy thud and shot to the surface, gasping, shaking my long hair.

I closed my eyes and let the water flush around me. The wind was sweet in the trees. I could hear my coffee simmering, and, in a moment, I'd climb out to throw in four packets of cream, one of sugar. Oh Lord, I thought, do I *like* this?

"I be VC, you a dead man, Irish."

Alarm ran over me, and shame: it was Ransom. Of all people, Sergeant Ransom. I looked up at him mournfully. "I let down my guard. Just for a minute."

"Cain't have no minutes, Irish."

"I know." I crawled onto the bank, ridiculous in my nakedness, my cherished solitude now as remote as my childhood. I reached for the canteen cup and knocked it over.

"We call you on the radio but it gone dead. You the sergeant now. Men depend on you."

"Dietrich was supposed to change the batteries. But—but— it's *my* fault." Had I ever seen him relax? He seldom spoke, and I forgot he was there, sometimes, until I needed him, until they fired. Looking at him, calm, selfless, neither a hero nor a coward, pulled me through. "I'm sorry."

"We been kicking back, too," he said, smiling. I had never seen him smile. His eyes bulged slightly, and he turned to look down the paddy, where second squad stood near the Renault truck—too far away to laugh at me. "But we gots to move out now."

"Where we going?"

"Bravo chase some snipers into Sông Trì Village. I think we going to help 'em out. We going to rendezvous with Captain Bell, then we all walk in, get some hot chow. I know where *I* go."

"It's your last day! You're going home!"

That was the second time I saw him smile.

In my mind I could fit the area onto a map, but it was unfamiliar land all the same, and when we stepped onto the road it was as though I'd never been there. I knew that in one direction lay the river, and the bridge to Indian Country, while in the other was the village and the base.

Ransom was still platoon leader, of course, but he happily deferred to me. I called Captain Bell.

"This is Bandit. You get those papers, Six?"

"I did, sir. Thank you, sir."

He gave me his coordinates. "Bravo's squared away with the bad guys. Rendezvous you me in the romeo trees, we'll hitch a ride and get some chow at HQ."

We trudged up the red road. Far west was a treeline, and a series of huts for making charcoal, that I recognized. Ahead, the road should curve.

Detroit let several men go around him, then turned to Ransom. "Where we going, my man? We gonna link up with Bravo?"

Ransom gestured toward me.

I shrugged. "Bravo headed 'em off at the pass so I don't think so. Bell says to meet him in the rubber plantation. We'll take a truck on in, get some hot chow."

"Then what?" Detroit asked.

Ransom waved his arms up and down. "Fly away."

Detroit slapped Ransom's hand. "Well, *you*. Gonna miss you, my man."

"Miss you, too, brother."

Rubber trees closed in on either side. There were gashes in their trunks and wooden buckets strewn about, where villagers had been working. A man in second squad pulled away strips of sap, worked them into a ball, threw the ball forward. Louie turned, as if instinctively, to leap and catch it. He threw it back but it bounced and rolled along in the dry red dirt of the road, turning red, too.

Dietrich glared. "Where the fuck *are* we, Irish?" Sims had slowed, and looked back for direction. I grabbed the radio operator's handset, realizing now that the road which had seemed familiar was a kilometer or so wrong. It was like coming in the back way of some huge building, when, for months, I'd come in the front way. I was about to press the handset button, but now Bell was shouting at me. "Bandit 6, Bandit 6, this is Bandit. Where the fuck are you?"

"We—we thought we would link up—"

"Negative, our element is back in the wire, we caught a ride. Put Ransom on."

It wasn't my fault. I'd guided us to within fifty meters of the coordinates he'd given me, right down the road. Ransom smiled apologetically, took the handset, and I stepped back.

I walked into the rubber trees and urinated into one of the buckets. I rolled a piece of sap in my fingers and tried to flip it away, but it clung. What was *that?*

Bobbing my head left and right, I could see a hint of orange. It was an odd shade, nearly red, and nothing within miles had that color except the tile roof of the temple. I was right! We'd come in from the south, rather than the east. And no, we'd never been on this road. The coordinates had been wrong, not me. "Hey!" I called back. "I know where we—"

There was an explosion and the quick rattle of machine guns. Back on the road, the men milled, leaped for the cover of the trees. "Not us! Not us!" I shouted.

Ransom was beside me. "You see?"

"We're north of the temple. There's that dirty little creek, and the charcoal smelters, and the steam bath—"

"Bravo backed 'em in there. Bell says go."

We scurried down the hill. The firing lifted and fell; finally, we could see them, Bravo behind charcoal smelters and the stockade full of scrawny cattle, firing into the steam bath. The steam bath's windows had been shot out and no fire returned. The back door was open and smoke rolled out. The cattle bawled, and strained against the pole fence.

Detroit stared. "Weird shit. Ain't no VC in the village."

"Tracked 'em down," Jim Cole said.

Ransom nodded. "Run in there, thought they was safe."

As if it had been fueled with gasoline, a grass fire leaped up beside the building. "Them cattle!" Dietrich said.

"Cocoa," said Screwy Louie. I didn't understand for an instant, then remembered. He meant the madame herself, the Cambodian, called Cocoa because of her dark skin. Apparently, he knew her intimately.

Sims looked from Louie to me. "Cowkie!"

"Oh, no," I said. "No, Sims—"

He began running.

"Hey, troop!" Dietrich shouted, and ran after him. We all followed, sliding down into the rancid creek. There were rises of mud and Sims fell, went skidding around a bend and an eroded bank. We drew up together and crept along the bank, hanging low, watching. Fire rolled along the wall of the steam bath and caught the strewn hay in the cattle pen. The cattle bumped frantically against the opposite fence.

"Irish!" Dietrich shouted. "We can't let them cows—"

"Stay where you are," I said, waving him down. Despite the panic in the air I knew no one had to get hurt. Whoever was inside the steam bath was trapped.

But Dietrich was bound to save those cattle. Detroit grabbed his leg but he kicked free. He ran forward, leaning low into the smoke, to raise the pole holding the gate. The cattle shoved through the rolling smoke, flopped down the bank, and ran along the creek. Two ran the opposite way, through the crossfire and behind the utility shed. There was a burst of fire from the steam bath and Dietrich dropped.

Now Sims ran forward. "Stay down, stay down!" I screamed. Would no one listen? Sims drew fire and dropped, sliding, behind a water trough.

The lieutenant in Bravo stood up. It was that damned Dranow. Did he have orders to preside over ruin? *"Chieu hoi!"* he called out, meaning surrender, but new AK fire popped out of the smoke. Dranow nodded. His gunner came to one knee, balancing a LAW on his shoulder. The rocket sailed the little distance through the doorway. A portion of the roof caved in and fire leaped along the tin. Voices came from within, in a high, almost feminine whine: *"Dùng ban! Dùng ban!"*

Three shapes ran out into the smoke. Detroit and the Bravo gunner cut them down as they appeared, at the instant someone shouted that they were women. There was another explosion. The back wall fell and the roof lurched downward, but held at an angle. Ammunition began cooking off in the fire and rounds whizzed.

It was over.

A jeep drew up with Colonel Drake, Captain Bell, and a major from Intelligence. The Colonel motioned to Dranow, who trotted over and saluted.

Bell spoke to Ransom. He glanced at Dietrich's body. "Sergeant Donnelly, what the hell?"

"I couldn't stop him, he—"

The Major tried to talk to the old women, then to a farmer, then to the children who had gathered at a distance. How could he explain the dead women, innocent at least of politics? The children ran from him. He shouted after them in Vietnamese.

We wrapped Dietrich in his poncho liner. He was heavy and it took four of us to put him in the jeep. We drew back. No one had liked him and there wasn't anything to say.

Dietrich, scourge of lizards.

Sims was walking toward the utility shed that so far had escaped the fire. Lord, I thought, and hurried after him. He disappeared into the dark inside.

I looked down and a woman lay at my feet. It was Madame Cocoa, whom I'd seen once alive, beautiful, haughty Cocoa, but half her head was gone and she wasn't anything anymore. I kept waiting for shock to come, but it didn't. All I thought was that, dead, a woman looked about like a man.

"Cowkie?" Sims moaned.

She wasn't there. Her mother was dead from the crossfire, but Cuc Hoa was nowhere near.

I turned around and there weren't any people now, no one but soldiers. More rounds cooked off, like firecrackers.

Ransom, head low, sat on the hood of the jeep. The Colonel, looking grim, motioned to his driver.

Ransom looked up at me and then his eyes dropped like something slowly falling. I never saw him again.

9

Farewell to Paradise

OVER THE THANKSGIVING weekend Wombat and his squad were running two soft drink and coffee stands at rest stops north of Tampa. It was my last chance to see them before I returned to Missouri.

Wombat had told us that charitable organizations could make as much as five thousand dollars in a single night. "First thing: Put up a sign that says, 'Donations accepted.'"

"And look pitiful?" I asked.

"You shouldn't have any trouble there."

Wombat had a story of parachuting into North Vietnam. They were in a spy plane filled with electronic equipment designed to catch stray radio impulses, track missiles, etc. Ten kilometers north of the DMZ they hit a cloud of flak and both engines caught fire. The captain pushed the destruct button because of all the secrets on board, aimed the plane for the sea, and then everyone bailed out.

There they were in the dense jungle. Wombat regrouped with four others and they hiked out, following a wild river. Several times they were pursued. One man died of fever and another was lost to quicksand. A beautiful peasant woman gave them food and clothing. Barely alive, they staggered into a marine firebase, where the soldiers mistook them for the enemy, and nearly wasted them.

The Deer Hunter, I thought, by way of *The Right Stuff* by way of *Mission: Impossible.* Wombat told his stories well, but sometimes a look came into his eyes that hinted he knew we were playing games. Even now he sauntered forth, waving his thumbs in imaginary suspenders. "Pil-grum," he said. "I want you to take command of that Pepsi trailer."

So far we were the only ones there. I looked across the stream of traffic, glimmering in the afternoon sun, toward the other rest stop. I nodded soberly. "All right, Cap'n," I said. "Somebody has to do it."

He scribbled the number for a nearby pay phone. "This is for commo checks."

"Roger that, sir." He liked that, the "sir," so I threw in a salute.

I drove to the interchange, back on the other side, and opened the stand. I propped up some paintings, too: Wombat's flag draping a casket, and one of Sanchez's of vets in wheelchairs, playing basketball. I thought how pleased Sanchez would be if we sent him a little check.

I had one customer as I was working, a truck driver from West Virginia. He stared at our brochure, then looked doubtfully at me. "You were over there?"

"Sure was."

"Rambo!"

"No, not me."

"You seem like a real normal guy."

"Thanks, I—"

"They gonna fly it in?"

"What?"

"Your turkey dinner! For turkey day!" He laughed at his own joke, then dug in his pockets and threw all his change into the bucket. He walked off, laughing, and when he turned out with his truck gave thumbs up.

An old couple slowly approached, in an ancient Chrysler with Ontario plates. They sat in the car several minutes, staring at the trailer, at me and my long, anachronistic hair. Finally they emerged and walked carefully by, not looking at me, the woman clinging to the man. I called Wombat.

"Read you loud and clear, guy. How you me?"

"Lickin chicken."

"Any customers?"

"Made a dollar."

"Real fine, soldier, real fine. Carry on."

Wombat was probably right that I looked pitiful. How could it have been otherwise for a stranger in a strange land, recovering from divorce? Yet I couldn't fault Paradise. My father's example was correct. A long embrace of solitude, and two years without winter, had cleared the air.

The vets had offered solace. A man needs a good woman if he needs one, but there are times when it is prudent to hide out among one's own sex. As I poured coffee and scooped ice, and delivered the group spiel about the noble sacrifices veterans had made, the last thing on my mind was a female.

She wore thick glasses and her hair, which she'd drawn into a ponytail, was long and unruly. She had fair skin which had taken a sunburn. Her car, a battle-scarred Sunbird, shuddered as she drove up, and dieseled half a minute after she'd cut the engine.

She was like that, too: slightly out of time. She stepped from the car gracefully and would have turned any man's head but then, on that smooth asphalt, she stumbled, caught herself, and walked ahead so purposefully that the timid little girl showed through.

She joined me at the Pepsi stand, announcing she was there to help the Vietnam vets through the weekend. As she finished her speech her eyes leaped with surprise, as they read mine. She ducked her head but brought it up again with a brave smile. For some of us simply greeting the day takes courage. "I'm Silvie. Dawson's friend."

"Oh, right," I said, nodding. "The marine." Our hero, I thought, the man with the Navy Cross. I wondered if it would do any good to mention my Purple Heart, but I had never stooped so low. "Good for Dawson," I murmured.

"Oh," Silvie said neutrally, but drawing out the word. "Oh, I don't know."

In a few minutes, when *he* arrived, Silvie ran to throw her arms around him, and look up at him almost worshipfully, as if he were some kind of cult leader. In fact, he did go to survivalist camps, sometimes, though the end of the Cold War had left him without obvious enemies. Still, he was ready.

The Navy Cross was the only significant thing that had ever happened to him and he venerated it night and day. He drove a van he'd painted camouflage, wore camouflage fatigues. A bull rattler's skin hung over his rearview mirror. He lived somewhere among the palmettos and cypresses of Pasco County, where black bears still roam, and his van was full of guns and knives and physical fitness equipment. He was all nerves, marching quickly, gracefully, from station to station of our little bivouac, turning about with a sort of martial dance step.

But he seldom spoke, unless it was to defend our role in Vietnam so long ago. That time we'd argued in Orlando was forgiven and forgotten. He and I kept our respectful distance, old soldiers in a vanquished army.

Gene Cooley arrived. I hadn't seen him since the Masquerade Ball, and he had gained still more weight. I wondered how I could walk, but life had improved for him, even so. After five hearings, his disability status had been upgraded, if that's the word, from forty to one hundred percent, and now he had his own apartment.

He propped an American flag on the trailer and it fell down and he spent half an hour securing it with duct tape and binder twine, breathing heavily all the while. Then he patrolled the perimeter of the rest stop, slow-moving as a turtle. He peered into the swamp and walked among the big trucks and staggered in the sand along the Interstate. I understood: you had to secure your area, make up some rules, prepare yourself in the event of attack.

Satisfied at last, Gene popped a tape of the Doors into his car stereo, sat on a beach chair behind the trailer, and begged a beer from Dawson. He slurped it down and started on a pack of Winston Lights. I sat beside him for a while. His music eliminated any need for talk: Jim Morrison, Eric Clapton, and all of a sudden

Barry Sadler, plunging into the sky with his "Ballad of the Green Berets."

Meanwhile Silvie gave every weary traveler a smile. She would smile, I thought, as you steadily broke her heart.

Silvie and Dawson moved nicely together, an unlikely perfect couple, as if she were the only person on earth for whom he could soften those hard edges, or she were the only person who could see that those edges weren't really so hard. And he caught her little vulnerabilities, made her less tentative—ah, yes, I thought, there was hope for us. When I might have concluded that, in love, only money mattered, here was a woman who would give all she had to a man with nothing.

Around ten the Marine set up a gas grill. I sat eating hamburgers and Hydrox cookies and the potato salad that Gene Cooley had brought, and which it would have been the deepest imaginable offense not to sample. I swilled it down with Stroh's from cans, and then we lay on the hillside in the warm night under the big Florida moon, drinking, swapping combat stories, swatting black flies that swarmed out of the swamp behind. Truckers pulled in to catch some sleep and when they woke stumbled over, at two or three in the morning. They grabbed coffee and a handful of cookies before heading on to Orlando or Ft. Pearce.

The janitor came out and stood near the grill long enough that Dawson made him a hamburger.

"How you like your job?" I asked.

"It's a hard job." He sighed and shook his head tragically. "Long weekend like this, we'll go through five cases a toilet paper."

The Marine smiled thinly. "That's a lot of asses."

The janitor looked off across the highway. "People don't realize. You get some characters. I don't mean you people. That thing over there, it was a real tragedy, but nobody blames you men."

I glanced at the Marine. He stood with his chin in profile against the moon, proud yet inscrutable, a fit subject for one of Wombat's paintings.

The janitor took a swallow of coffee. "Sometimes I say to Rita, if it wasn't for I'd mess up my retirement, we'd pull up stakes and head back to Tennessee. Nothing down here no more. Tuesday night, maybe seven-eight in the evening, we had these two nigra boys come up from Tampa. I thought, they look suspicious, but like I say to Rita, man should mind his own business, and anyhow you see so many. They sat out there smoking dope in an old beat-up three-quarter-ton International. They was just waiting, and finally this old woman from New York City pulls up, and they run quick and get her purse, I guess she had a *wad* a money. And they lit out south. I called the po-lice, but see, that's why they was *on* this side, they's an interchange down two miles and they can get off before the highway patrol runs 'em down."

"Is there a lot of that kind of thing?" asked the Marine, dropping his head at last, and looking stern.

"What you see mostly is the kids making their dope deals."

"Helluva world," the Marine said.

"Seems to me," the janitor said, "it gone to hell ever *since* that war."

It was four in the morning. Silvie had gone to sleep in the van, so whatever elegance or mystery the night held was gone. Gene lay snoring in his chair; sometimes, he'd stir slightly, gas would rumble in his belly, and he'd belch. The Marine's conversation, such as it was, grew impatient. His eyes drifted toward the van.

Even the Interstate was quiet, and for an hour we'd had only one customer, a trucker who held out his thermos like a beggar seeking alms. Then, as the Marine spun on heel, and I rose from my chair and headed for the knoll where I'd thrown out my sleeping bag, a white Mercedes two-door with tinted glass streaked in, trailing smoke.

Gene woke, as an old infantryman always will, and the three of us jumped like a pit crew. A woman—a blonde in a white, low-cut summer dress and white stockings—leaped from the Mercedes, saw us, made her mute, helpless female appeal. In an instant you could tell, though the fire was real enough, and the damsel's distress was real enough, that her *ploy* was—well, that it was an act.

So much the better. The Marine, when he saw the car coming, had run to his van to grab a small CO_2 extinguisher. Gene was trying to open the hood. "Yes, ma'am, yes, ma'am, stand back, ma'am," he said, as the lady in white stamped her feet and turned about in panic. I ran over, too, but as always my role was not the hero's. The Marine took the glories. I slid behind the wheel and pulled the latch so that Gene could raise the hood, and the Marine mount his assault on the carburetor.

Dawson doused the fire quickly, then stepped back, almost as if he expected applause. "Oh, you're just *won*derful," said the woman in white. "I don't know what I'd have done if—"

"See if we can get her started again," Gene muttered. He was shorter than the woman and kept glancing up at her. He tucked in his shirttail and gave her a smile. She returned his smile but then stepped over near the Marine and touched his arm, and brushed his chest for whatever dirt he might have encountered in the course of heroism. He dropped his head and stood almost at attention, as though awaiting her next assignment.

Silvie climbed from the van and walked slowly over, looking nearsighted and frail without her glasses, and overwhelmed, perhaps, by the glamour of the visitor. She stared at her rival and put her arm around Dawson. The woman edged toward me, second choice.

"Out late," I said.

I must have seemed sarcastic, for her eyes widened slightly, and quickly compressed. She bit her lip. "Well ... I had to be in Ocala for a ... party. And I couldn't get away, couldn't get away— you know how it is."

"You some kind of performer?"

She smiled distantly, as if she were too well bred for a comment. Like Jacqueline, I thought. I was glad I'd been immunized.

"Crank it, Irish," Gene called out irritably. He'd been leaning over the engine, cursing the metric system. Grateful for something to do, I slipped into the car and turned the key. The engine started and I raced it until it ran smoothly.

The woman took a few steps toward Gene, applauding.

"Used to work on tractors," he announced, dropping the hood with authority now, and hulking around the car. I got out so he could hold the door for her.

"Thank you, sir," the woman said, with a sweeping gesture. She pulled a red shawl around her tanned shoulders, gathered her skirt, and slid behind the wheel once more. "Mmmm," she said, and touched Gene's cheek with her fingers. The muscles where his scars were jumped.

"Nice little car," he said, panting. "I wonder if—maybe—you oughtta drive a little slower."

"I'll do that." She put the Mercedes in gear and edged forward.

"You're the most beautiful woman ...," Gene began, but his voice faltered, as the woman in white gave no clue she heard.

"Your husband," she called out to Silvie. "He's a real hero!"

"I think they're *all* heroes," Silvie said.

I was so weary I could hardly climb to the knoll and sleep. But I felt good about myself, perhaps because I had belonged somewhere for a little while.

Sleep came like a steep fall, and I was with my father when he was a young man, still, and I was hardly in school. Dad was making me a bow out of Osage Orange, the hardest and toughest wood in the United States, wood that always springs erect. We were out in the shop on a winter day and the barrel stove was sizzling, but the cement floor was cold and the wind battered the windows. And, somehow, I took my father's place, whittling patiently at that bow with a spoke shave, and the boy looking up at me was Dale.

I awoke there on the hillside to the birds singing with dawn, my legs stiff, this foreign land of Florida already hot, and sitting by my side was Silvie.

"Good morning, Irish," she said. "I have something for you." She held out a cup of coffee and a Styrofoam container with an egg sandwich in it.

"Dawson bought it for you. Is it all right?"

"Sure. Thanks a lot, Silvie. Where's the—where is Dawson?"

"He went to Tampa for ice."

"You sleep?"

"A little. After all the excitement—"

"Did he?"

"Did he ... yes, he slept awhile. He doesn't sleep much."

"Ever vigilant."

"What?"

I stood slowly on my aching knees, and kicked out one foot and then the other to make the blood work. I was too old to sleep on the ground. "Is it pretty good, the two of you?"

She blushed. "He found me, I was coming apart. He—"

"You see that truck there?" No more Volvo: I had a brand-new Toyota truck. Everyone should identify those problems that can be solved with money. Then all you have to do is find some money.

Silvie smiled, and I wanted to grab her and run, Marine or no Marine. "Sure. Dawson says you're going back home."

"Let's take a ride. Let's take a long ride."

She laughed. "Where to, bigshot?"

"Alaska!"

"You're terrible. You're not serious."

"Of course not," I said, looking away. I couldn't find words. There had flashed in my mind an old picture of my mother, when she was slim and quite beautiful but still a child of the Depression, worries tugging down at her eyes.

"Nice," I said at last. "That he has somebody like you."

"And I have somebody like *him*." She brought up her chin. "Irish, if I didn't—"

"Right." We walked toward the Pepsi trailer and I had more coffee and a handful of cookies.

The phone rang. "This is Wombat, how you read?"

"Gotcha lima charles."

"Make boocoo dinero, did you?"

"Not quite two hundred. You?"

"Same-same. We got three more days. Talk to you later, big guy."

There was a flurry of customers and Silvie and I worked side by side. Without looking at me, she said, "Did you win any medals over there?"

"Not me, Silvie. I'm a boy wonder, not a hero."

She grinned. Gene Cooley woke and headed for the bathroom, tucking in his shirttail as he walked. The janitor shuffled by, nodded shortly, went home. Dawson returned with ice and twelve dozen doughnuts, and managed what was for him a big smile.

I was headed north again, more or less repaired, ready for fatherhood if not for romance. It occurred to me that this was Thanksgiving Day.

10

World of Hurt

WHEN THE COLONEL'S jeep pulled away with Ransom I turned and headed for the utility shed. I stood in the doorway with my eyes adjusting; crossfire had doused the light. I saw the TV, a trunk, a chair. Then I realized that Sims was staring at me, his eyes slits of red in the shadows.

He held the old woman in his lap. She looked unhurt, but soon I saw that her forehead glistened from an abrasion, like a first-degree burn where one layer of skin peels away. "Norman," I said. "I'm sorry."

He leaned against me. "Where's Cuc Hoa?"

"We have to go, Norman. There's nothing you can do here. We have to—"

"I have to find my wife!"

I tried to drag him outside but he threw me against the wall. I hit a pole with a nail in it where a blouse was hanging, and the nail gouged along my neck where the boil had burst. I leaned against the wall, fatigue running through me, and fought for breath. Everything smelled of blood. "Norman—"

"I'll stay here, I'll *live* here. I'll be a gook!"

I grabbed his arm. He followed me for a step and then hit me in the chest. I drew my elbows before my face and backed out as he jabbed at me.

My platoon had gathered in a patch of shade, while, behind them, Bravo was cleaning up the mess. A soldier dragged one of the bodies by its heels, let it fall.

"Detroit," I called. "I can't—"

He slid by me in the doorway. "Aw," he said. "That too bad. That too bad, Jesus. They didn't mean it, Norman, they didn't mean it you *know* that, man, don't you know? Don't you know that, hon? You c'mon now, it be all right. You come on with your friends."

"Cowkie … "

Detroit led him out. "We gonna find her, man. She *fine*. Don't you worry!"

Everyone in Bravo stared at us. Dranow, his chin strap buckled, looked downright frightening. He stared at Sims, jerked up his head in acknowledgment, and wheeled to bark an order.

We hurried up the road, Sims leaning against Detroit. It was quitting time on the base. The people coming home didn't look at us as we passed, and I knew that already the word had spread.

"Those fuckers!"

"Norman—" I said. "You don't talk like that. Not you."

"Bastards!" He flushed red. "Dranow, that sonuvabitch!"

"Norman—"

"I'm all right!" He tore away from Detroit and marched ten steps with an exaggerated rigidity, as if he'd learned to walk in a drill team. Then he dropped into his place in the file, swung his rifle, bore his head low.

At two in the morning he was still raving.

"I tried to be a good soldier, Irish. I tried so hard to be good at this? I wasn't ever any good at sports. I didn't wanta come over here, you know? I thought the war was wrong! Only then I went to basic, I thought the war was *right!* But I didn't think it was like this. I didn't know they just killed people all the time, just went in the village and killed people. Did you find Cowkie?"

"Tomorrow. We're going on patrol, I'll look through the village. I'll find her."

"Where is she?"

"She's fine."

"Can I see her?"

"Not tonight. You need to sleep."

"Why did they kill all those women?"

If you counted Cuc Hoa's mother Bravo Company killed six females, four males, and two persons unidentifiable after the fire. That was a kill ratio of twelve to one if you allowed that the four prostitutes were unfriendly. How did you compute Dietrich, who had been a kind of noncombatant?

Battalion wasn't interested in any count whatever. Colonel Drake spent his next days fielding questions from reporters, explaining himself to generals, and apologizing to Vietnamese. In causing us to kill civilians, the VC had shown real genius, he said. That was the kind of crazed and inhumane force we were dealing with. Nothing, of course, could make up for the loss of innocent lives.

Even so, one hundred bags of rice, seized from an NVA cache in Cambodia, would find their way into the village larder.

Luckily, Bravo actually *had* killed some VC, but still it seemed odd that they had continued firing once the cornered men had cried, *"Dùng ban!"* There was talk of an inquiry, but in the end, as everyone knew in the first place, it was wisest to let the matter drop. There weren't any rules in a firefight. No one paused to contemplate politics.

"It was an accident," I said. "That damn Dranow. There *were* some VC; they wasted one of our guys. Bravo wanted to run 'em right into the ground, and they did, that's all. The VC opened up, they were good, they *knew* there were friendlies there. They wanted to make it look like Americans are evil."

"We *are* evil," Sims said. "We're just like the French."

He drew KP for several weeks. It wasn't meant as permanent duty this time, for Sims had become a field soldier. But the cook had requested him, and, perhaps, there had been a decision made

somewhere, that with Cuc Hoa out of the way the best place for
Sims was back in mess.

Battalion flew us in one morning about nine, and Detroit
and I hurried to the mess hall. It was too late for breakfast but,
sometimes, you could tell a sad story and talk your way in, to wolf
down cold biscuits and grapefruit juice. I banged on the door.
There was a rustling inside, and, finally, an eye peeked through the
blind.

"Hiya, Irish!"

We stepped onto the concrete where Sims had romanced
Cuc Hoa beneath the parachute, and he handed us each a cup of
coffee. As I stood wondering what to say he ran around the corner,
came back rolling a great wooden spool. He was gone again, and
returned with two chairs.

"How's our hero?" Detroit asked.

Sims shook his head energetically, as though heroism were
not something civilized people discussed, and disappeared yet
again. We drank coffee and Detroit lit a Salem. "What you do in
Bangkok?" I asked him.

He threw back his head and blew smoke. "They gots this
little room, where you look down from the balcony. They gots this
one-way mirror kinda like, where you can see them only they
cain't see you, and you sit up there and pick out the old lady you
wants. So I pick one."

"Need a system like that back home."

"Shee-ut. Womens never let you."

Sims returned with a cloth from one of the tables reserved
for officers, and a bouquet of plastic flowers.

Detroit laughed. "Uptown, babe."

Sims brought us pancakes and eggs. He held a green towel
over his arm, stepped back with a flourish, bowed.

"Nice, Norman," I said. "Thanks a lot."

"Thank you, babes."

Sims beamed. He shoved salt and syrup near, walked off a
few steps, stood with his hands behind him. He went after bowls
of crushed pineapple.

"I ain't ate this good since I was in Bangkok," Detroit said. "You got it made in the shade, Norman."

Sims grinned and drew up a chair. "I used to come out here, I'd talk to Cowkie."

I swallowed hard. "Norman—"

"Listen to me, Irish! One time, when everybody was gone, I set it up just like this, with the tablecloth and the flowers and a chair for Cowkie, and I made tea! 'Would you like some tea, dear?' I said, and she said, *'Tôi can nuóc chè,'* and I said, 'Some sugar?' and she said, 'Yes, thank you very much,' and then I looked all around—Irish, Detroit—and nobody was there. All of a sudden, I stopped. I knew she wasn't there."

"Yeah," Detroit said.

"I was sad! But I knelt down right there, and I said, 'Lord, if you don't mean for us to get married, if it's not your will, then I don't want it, either.' Some things in this world, we just can't help. There are wicked men in this world! I know when I'm beat!"

"You ain't beat by a long ways," Detroit said. "You fucked up, but you ain't *shot* up."

"Don't ever say you're beat, Norman."

He dropped his eyes. "It's those guys, like you, Irish, only you're a good guy, who go to school. They run the world. And you know what I decided? I decided I want to go to school. Is Oral Roberts a good college, Irish?"

"Sure." I recalled the place: garish, oddly colored buildings meant to look futuristic when they were built, but, with the passing of years, coming to resemble the set of a cheap science fiction movie. "*Great* school."

He handed me an envelope. "Here."

It was his poker winnings. "What?"

"You give it to her, Irish. You tell her—you tell her it's all I can do."

We borrowed the company typewriter and banged out a letter to the apostles in Tulsa. Sims had been there once and driven by the college. The town was dripping with money in those days, and the school was young and untainted by scandal. He'd had worse ideas.

He worked hard at the mess hall. He didn't talk much, but he was cheerful. He didn't have friends except for what few old ones remained in the platoon, but he spent his free time reading or playing games at the Red Cross Club. He had scheduled an R&R to Sydney. Perhaps it was even correct to say that the army had made a man of him.

I wasn't there when it happened. My platoon was in Indian Country, had been for a week.

The chaplain entered the mess hall, skirting the long line outside, which was the privilege of his rank. Several officers at the Colonel's table waved at him and he called out, "Hey, Bob! Got some news."

The chaplain did nothing offensive, nothing more than usual, at least. Nothing at all! The menu was spaghetti and meatballs; he filled his plate. Sims came from the kitchen with a platter of garlic bread. The chaplain took a piece and put it down again in contempt, but it was ritual contempt. "Your bread's hard, soldier," he said.

He looked at Sims but didn't see him. Sims was not a person but a position, a slot, meriting neither a compliment nor an insult. The chaplain's remark meant nothing. How can you insult furniture? No doubt, had his gaze lingered an instant longer, the chaplain *would* have recognized Norman, and seen him shrinking back. But he simply turned, breadless, toward his friends, and started across the floor.

How could you cause a man the kind of woe the chaplain had caused Sims and then not recognize he existed? It must have seemed to Sims that the chaplain had belittled Cuc Hoa in a final, unendurable way. Sims vaulted over the table, scattering the garlic bread.

He leaped on the chaplain's back. The plate fell and broke; spaghetti slopped along the buffed floor. Before anyone even realized what was happening Sims was on top of the chaplain, choking him.

Would he have killed him?

In any event, the man with the Silver Star had assaulted an officer. Not merely an officer, but a man of God! Colonel Drake pushed back his chair, leaped, and slugged Norman. The cook, screaming at the top of his lungs, ran to the Colonel's side, and together they pulled Sims away.

Slowly, the chaplain sat. No question, he recognized Norman now. He rubbed his neck. Blood rushed to his face. He seemed more disbelieving than angry, and then he seemed regretful.

Next day, he begged the Colonel to go easy.

Norman wasn't angry, either. He was like a man cured of all ambition, all jealousy, and any least inclination to violence. He seemed almost indifferent when the MPs came, and handcuffed him, and drove him to the stockade.

At dawn the rain stopped. I'd lain listening to it all night, finally giving up on sleep and sloshing downhill to company headquarters. Two men, anonymous in the shrouds of their ponchos, trudged past me to the mess hall door, but it was a few minutes early for breakfast, still. Long Binh Jail, I thought, or simply LBJ in tribute to our leader. It couldn't be.

Somewhere, a big Wisconsin generator hummed to life.

Around the greenline, bulky figures stood silhouetted on the morning sky, drying themselves around fires of C-ration cardboard and cottonwood ammunition crates. As the light strengthened the individual faces seemed new, or, rather, you had forgotten them and they surprised you with their familiarity, like cousins and uncles who had arrived from a far state.

Hickman nodded hello and I poured a cup of his range coffee, sat in the corner biting down on grounds. There was a percolator somewhere, but he was Old Army, and preferred bad coffee. He reminded me of my dad. When I was a kid he'd make coffee atop a wood stove on a cold Sunday, then sit through the afternoon, reading Ernest Haycox.

Hickman wrote for a while in his neat, laborious script. Finally, he sighed and snapped out the desk lamp. Light had come, and shammers limped down the hill like so many lepers, reporting for morning formation. Across the way, I could see the lighted top halves of men, carrying trays inside the mess hall.

Hickman sealed the papers and handed them across. "You don't have to do this, Donnelly."

"I want to, First Sergeant." *Sure. I want to take him to Long Binh Jail.*

Hickman reached into his desk drawer and brought out a .45 with a holster.

"I don't think I'll—"

"Regulations, Donnelly."

He walked me to the door. "Manjack getting off easy," he said at last. "The Colonel could have—"

"It's not like he's some criminal, First Sergeant."

"The army goes by its rules, you know that. Or it ain't the army."

Sims was sitting in the jeep when I reached the pad. He lifted his handcuffs and grinned.

The two MPs were leaning against the grill, smoking and drinking coffee, but when they saw me they grew curt and admonitory and handed me a release to sign. I felt odd standing with them, and wearing the .45. When we had climbed onto the helicopter I freed Sims's hands.

"Thanks, Irish!"

"I can't believe they put those things on you. Are you okay? Did you get some breakfast?"

"I had a banana."

The door gunner eyed us glumly. I recognized him from long before, on Firebase Sheila after the battle, but neither of us spoke. His eyes dropped to the jungle ulcers along my neck.

We passed over the rubber plantation and then followed the river as we climbed, until everything seemed smoky and remote. The wet jungle was grand and wild under the rising sun, but in any direction I looked there were bomb craters, in neat, long rows like an experiment in irrigation. "Thirty days, what's that?" I shouted.

"They don't count it, it isn't fair!"

He meant that when he returned he'd still have the same amount of time to serve.

"Can I see your .45?"

I handed it to him without hesitation. The door gunner frowned, then turned on his perch and stared out again, sipping from his coffee.

Sims pantomimed shooting things, blowing at the imaginary smoke. "How many days, Irish?"

"Fifty-one."

"You think they got TV there?"

"In LBJ?" I laughed. "They won't let you watch it, even if they do."

"Not even the moon shot?"

"God, Norman. I don't know."

"I mean, it's *his*tory, Irish."

We couldn't find the place at first. We went wandering among the quonset huts of Long Binh base, that stern officers' paradise, saluting madly, too scared to ask directions, a couple of hicks in the big city. Finally, as we stood by the library where four black men were painting a wall, we saw the President's jail—a tenement rising out of the hedge-lined walks, rosebushes, and grass so green it, too, seemed to adhere to regulations. "Is that it?"

The man he'd spoken to looked Norman up and down, then turned as if to ignore him. "They puts you in a Connex, white boy," he said, finally. "Sweat out your sins."

"You in there? What you do?"

The man shrugged and moved further away. The other men hadn't looked at us. We turned and walked straight for the entrance, and the man called out, "Be good, you get on the chain gang like me."

Everyone who went there, I thought, had a story. If a man's story was less subtle than Norman's, even if he was a true criminal, still there must have been a point when his fate could have gone another way. Suppose some other soldier had been serving spaghetti, and Norman was washing dishes. Destiny hung on where you stood at a particular moment, whether you were an instant early or late.

There we were, a few feet from one of history's saddest places. Nothing to it: a sign rose out of rows of sandbags announcing a weapons checkpoint, and beyond that was the fence with its layers of concertina wire. But the fence was scary. It was draped with green canvas so that you couldn't see within, or so prisoners couldn't see out.

"Maybe, maybe—I could have talked to the chaplain," I said. "I didn't think it would do any good. I'm sorry, Norman. This is—"

"You get outta here, I-rish! They'll put *you* in!"

He hit me on the shoulder and stepped forward, holding his Bible in one hand, his orders in the other. No, he wouldn't be able to watch Neil Armstrong walk on the moon, but he was probably right that the Bible was the one item they wouldn't take from him. Faith would get him through.

A guard jerked a thumb with ritual anger, and Norman disappeared through the nondescript entrance, hardly more than a tent flap. I backed away, studying the entrance from another angle, but it was a cunning place, and there was no divining its evils from the outside. I stumbled into someone, a major.

"Soldier!"

"What?"

Wrong response. "Are you authorized to be in this area, soldier?"

"Yes, sir." I handed him a copy of Norman's orders.

He returned them. "I wonder if you could tell me, young sergeant, what it is an enlisted man does when he meets an officer?"

I drew to attention and saluted.

"Very good. Drop for ten."

For an instant, I didn't recall the drill, but then I fell to the walk and pumped out pushups. In five he said, "That will do," and I rose and saluted again.

"Now, maybe you'll remember—," he began, but stopped when he met my eyes. I was crying.

"Carry on," he muttered, and strode away.

11

Student Days

DRIVING FROM FLORIDA I stopped off in Carthage, Missouri, where a friend of Cindy's had become a school superintendent. Chuck was my friend, too, and struggled to maintain his neutrality through the divorce. In my married days he was a bachelor librarian and I used to wonder if he was gay. Then he seemed to take Cindy's side and I concluded that he had designs on her. Maybe so, but nothing ever came of it. Or something did, and I was uninformed. Funny, in my old age, how little it mattered.

Chuck needed a junior high English teacher. Cindy told me. Once I'd have thought such a job to be the definition of hell, and Cindy and I would have argued all through the night how demeaning it was. No longer. "Yes. I want it."

Chuck shook his head, maybe not entirely assured the worst of times were behind me. "Your certificate's a little old, Patrick."

"*I'm* a little old," I said. "Think of me as, as—*seasoned*."

He smiled. "You'd have to take some refresher courses. This summer."

Sure, I said.

Could I advise the student newspaper? Absolutely. The annual? I looked forward to it. Coach girl's volleyball, too? No problem. I'd have buffed the gym floor, swabbed down the urinals, and painted the goddamn flagpole, if Chuck had asked.

We walked out of the building, planned a trip to St. Louis we both knew we'd never make, and shook hands. I walked toward my shiny new Toyota truck and knew that I'd come through.

So, after more than twenty years, I found myself back at the college where I'd met Trudy, signed up for two courses designed to make a modern man of me. I lay back on a bench in front of the college chapel and listened to a young woman play "Jesu, Joy of Man's Desiring," thankful the great hymn had arrived in a new generation.

The organist walked by, eyes downcast, and I cried out, "Beautiful!"

She seemed puzzled or even alarmed. "Bach," I added.

"Oh," she said sweetly. "Thank you."

I used to sit on this bench—the same bench with the same scars of love carved into it, painted over, carved again—waiting for Trudy to finish practicing her organ.

We'd have lunch right over *there*, at the Union. Phil Ochs and Pete Seeger came to sing, and Trudy and I embraced, stared into each other's eyes, contemplated peace.

I was a kid right out of the hills, still shaky from my mother's death and, so it seemed then, quite fatherless as well.

Trudy was the daughter of two lawyers on Long Island, a girl with all the curvature of a pencil but with a dark, knowing face, and a fanatic belief in love. She believed in it so strongly, in fact, that I wonder if she believed in it at all.

She would sit on the bed singing "Barbry Allen" as enchantingly as Joan Baez, but then she'd hit a sour note with the guitar and yell, "Fuck!" Perhaps Saint Joan did the same.

It was my hippy period, lasting all of three months. We'd get stoned and talk about *The Hobbit*. Or we lined up curious objects along her floor, and played choo-choo. On *Star Trek* nights our friends came over, like evangelicals gathered to hear a particularly hard-hitting evangelist.

I flunked all my classes, and, unlike Trudy, had no well-to-do family behind me. Secretly, as if I were beginning an affair, I drove home and volunteered for the draft. Ordinarily, that meant you had several months remaining of civilian life. I gave Trudy the news—that I'd been drafted, not that I'd volunteered.

"We could go to Canada," she said. The Quakers ran an underground from Seattle and could smuggle me into Vancouver. Was I that brave?

"Jobs are hard to find up there, Trudy. We—well, *I* could never come back."

"I thought you were committed!" she said. "I wish *I* were a man, so I could go to Canada. Or jail! I could go to jail! You—you *want* to fight." She was almost screaming.

And, not that I blamed her, she dumped me. I learned from her roommate that she had left the campus.

She had signed up with the Brethren Voluntary Service and gone to work in some hillbilly ghetto in eastern Kentucky. By the time I was in Sông Trì, with motives I couldn't begin to fathom, she wrote that she was pregnant by a coal miner's son. He himself was drafted and sent to Vietnam and, many years later, I discovered his name on the Wall.

Trudy seemed less interested in the fate of her lover than in their child. She planned to raise him or her according to golden, nonviolent principles derived, more or less, from popular songs. Wasn't love all you needed?

Money can be useful, too, and Trudy's parents had some. The child was given up for adoption and Trudy returned to school, and after that, she stopped answering my letters—precisely when Cindy began writing.

But Trudy was my first true love, and you can't underestimate the capacity of adolescents for melodrama. The night she left I wandered about all night convinced my life was at an end, and by morning was out on the highway, determined to hitchhike to Canada.

Somewhere west of Des Moines an Indian named Joe Buck gave me a ride on his Honda 305 Hawk. He'd worked all summer in Chicago on a new dormitory at Loyola, saved his money, and was headed back to the reservation in Idaho. Joe took me to Rock Springs, Wyoming, where I bought a bus ticket because it was miserably cold on the motorcycle. I had no gloves and my hands were freezing.

Over the years, when I told this story, I had to change Joe Buck's name to others that seemed more Native American—"Big Elk," or "Running Wolf." Sometimes, I left out that Joe was an Indian at all, but what people didn't believe was "Joe Buck." "Wasn't he the *Midnight Cowboy* character?" they'd ask, turning me into Ratso Rizzo.

In Seattle I stayed with the brother of a friend from college, a philosophy teacher at the University of Washington. He was vehemently opposed to the war and approved of the Friends who ran the underground to Vancouver.

The Quakers were extraordinary in every way. I rode across the border with a beautiful young woman, Sharon Kinkaid, a Canadian attending school in Seattle. The cover story was that I was her boyfriend, and she was taking me home to meet her parents.

Lies. Funny how people stopped me with "Joe Buck," the true part of the story, and bought all the rest. There was no beautiful Quaker girl, or maybe I *would* have gone to Canada. There was a professor active in the peace movement, but he didn't want me in his tiny house and soon made noises that if I was truly bound for Canada, I should get on with it.

Each day I promised him I'd visit the Friends' Center, and each day postponed it, wandering among the bookstores and head shops of the U. District, instead. One day, to get out of the rain, I stepped into a naval recruitment office, and nearly enlisted. Finally, for the first time in over a year, I called my father, and sure enough, my draft notice had arrived. I'd be inducted in twenty-one days.

But it was far more romantic, in the years that followed, to pretend that I went over the border. Once there, the full realization hit me that I would never see my friends again, nor the country, right or wrong, that I'd grown up in. Everyone liked this story, since many had themselves gone through similar, if less dramatic, moral agonizings.

I did at last go to the Friends' Center. I came quietly in the front door and stood for a while in the near-darkness, meditating. I seemed to be alone. Since it was a church, after all, I slipped into a pew and tried to muster religious feelings. Finally, a young man came from somewhere behind me, and asked if he could help. Older than me by ten years, but young.

"I want to go to Canada."

"Really," he said.

I waited for him to elaborate. I thought, "There! I've declared myself," and that matters were in his hands now, the Quaker on Duty.

"I've been drafted," I added hopefully.

"You feel strongly about this? What you're suggesting is a serious matter."

"I know ... *that.*"

"Tell you what." He wiggled his index finger in the "Come here, you" gesture I've always hated, and led me to a rack of paperbacks in the foyer. Most of them treated aspects of spirituality or the history of the Quakers, but there was one on taking a stand against war.

"Read this through, and come back in a couple of days."

"I thought—"

"It takes time to set these things up. It'll be like a carload of students, see. The pamphlet is one dollar."

"Well, I—"

"Helps defray the costs."

"I don't have—I didn't bring any money." This fellow and his pamphlet didn't go with the scene in my head, where there were federal agents at the door and a fast car, engine running, out back. "Seems like it should be free."

He frowned. "It's one dollar. I'm sorry."

My logic must have been that I wasn't about to pay a dollar to this schmuck who had no understanding of the hardships I had undergone, my commitment to peace, etc. Keeping my eyes low, I placed the pamphlet carefully on the rack, turned, and marched into the rain. I paused, as if the Friend would come after me. Then I hurried away, feeling like the fool that I was. I walked back to the university, left a note for my long-suffering host, grabbed a suitcase, and bought a ticket to Kansas City on the Great Northern.

That's the modest, sad, sorry truth, and the rest of it, how I was back in Seattle four months later, but as a soldier in advanced infantry training, hardly matters.

All the while I was in Vietnam I puzzled over why I rebelled at paying one dollar to be admitted to Canada. I'd come halfway across the country in the cause of peace, after all. How splendid if I had done what for years I claimed: gone over the border, then made a principled decision to return.

I disliked the Quaker on Duty, whose demand that I buy the pamphlet seemed to me monstrously petty. And I had my father's stubbornness, I must admit. He balked at paying out money for *anything*.

Still, after months of sitting on guard through the wee hours, I had to deny myself even this weak excuse. The truth was that the Quaker on Duty saw through me completely. A dollar for the pamphlet was his little field test of my sincerity. I failed, but then why had I gone West at all?

All my college friends were finding ways to evade the draft. It was unthinkable to go into the army, as, for more than a decade afterward, it was unthinkable to be a veteran. It wasn't *cool*.

Even more important, I was in love.

So, in an extraordinary demonstration of ambivalence, I went halfway. I tricked myself into thinking I'd go to Canada, when, at most, all I wanted was an adventure, or perhaps to make up with my girl.

Then for twenty years I lied about what I'd done, trying to make myself into a man of principle, or at least, an adventurer.

I did not *believe in the war,* that curious phrase of the time. But it was the greatest event of my generation, and I wanted to be part of it. I wasn't ambivalent. I wasn't wracked with moral agony. I intended to go to war from the first.

For fun, and since the catch-up courses I was taking were simple and I had time to kill, I went to the library and read through hundreds of alumni bulletins. Trudy was mentioned in 1982: she married a civil engineer and spent several years near the equator, in Iquitos, Peru. She had two girls, ages seven and ten. She was profiled again in 1991: a psychology professor at U.C. Davis, no husband mentioned.

There was a photograph. I stared at the woman, but not one square centimeter of skin, not her hair, her eyes, her lips, resembled the girl I had known.

I wondered if she had ever been curious about me. With these few clues I surmised that she was divorced, too. Maybe, some bleak night when the girls were with their father, she tracked down my number. She was one of those callers who think again when you answer, and click down the receiver.

Only a few months before, I couldn't find a girl with an ad in the paper. Now, they were everywhere: reckless, predatory single women; grave young married women; and, of course, divorced women—so plentiful they could constitute a census category. As if on holiday, they all were casual and friendly, and I had no competition, but I kept my tortured distance.

It's too bad that centuries of monks never found a way to make celibacy work. More men than you think would sign up.

Summer session finished, new job awaiting me, I drove past my old place. I pulled into the driveway and sat looking for signs of myself.

Except for the barn, there weren't any. Whoever bought the land bulldozed the foundations of the house and parked a trailer there, and planted Lombardy poplars down the lane. Lombardy poplars grow straight and tall in three years, and die in fifteen.

Probably long enough for this new cycle, and then another generation, still, would build on my ashes. So what? My musings on the impermanence of things only returned me to the fact a third of my life remained.

Enough time to find a reason to live it.

12

Officer Material

WE WERE MARCHING toward Indian Country when I found Cuc Hoa. She sat on the hillside above the river on the village side of the bridge, where a Bravo platoon, not Dranow's, lolled in ambush. There were three or four women with her I didn't know. As I neared her, a bare white ass rose up and down in the brush.

At first, Cuc Hoa looked through me. Was I a customer? She wore the dress Sims had bought her, and sat with her legs drawn up to showcase her thighs. She turned her head, and her beautiful hair, longer and glossier than ever, tumbled heavily. "You want good time?"

"Yeah. Let's steal a jeep and drive to Rangoon."

"Ranh...goon?" She tossed her hair. "Not make fun."

"Not pretend you don't know me."

"I know you, Charley Company. Killer."

I sighed. "I'm sorry about your mother, Cuc Hoa."

"Number one she *die!* She sick boocoo *time.*"

"I wish—"

"What you want, Charley? Boom-boom in bush? Number one good time, you like me?"

She stroked my cheek in mock-tenderness; I could feel the anger in her fingers. If I paid her and we had a number one time, would it be a sort of moral triumph? Maybe her attempt on me was revenge against Sims for being such a minor, such a power-less, American.

No, it was just business. I thrust out the envelope. "From Norman."

"Nor-*mahn!*"

"He saw your mother when she died, and—"

"Nor-mahn give me this?"

"He said it was all he could do."

"All?" She counted the money. The other women drew near as if the money were a piece of meat, and Cuc Hoa clutched the envelope to her breasts. "Piaster, piaster. Boocoo *dollar!*"

My platoon stared down from the bridge.

"You got a message?"

She opened her dress and slipped the envelope by her stomach. Her lips turned up in something like a smile. "Say good-bye, Irish."

Beyond the river, I plotted our way to a ruined village. There were no tunnels, no caches, and no people, nothing but a bleak, sun-baked sorrow. I could see where there had been a battle long ago, where the rockets had exploded and poisoned the soil, where the hooches had burned.

A rickety wharf ran out into the water. We sank two boats and one of Sergeant Crisco's men found a bloody, mildewed shirt. I squatted at the end of the wharf and looked across, raising my eyes to a high bluff. That was where Sims had shot his foot, half my life ago. I thought of him in jail—in jail, depending on how you looked at it, because of a prostitute.

A Loach buzzed out of the treetops and dipped like a hum-mingbird, twisting to hover midriver and face us. The door gunner dipped his Coke in salute. I should have been a door gunner, I thought. Good food. Clean bed.

Short life.

The pilot made radio contact and told me to follow him to a bunker complex. It was an odd request—his mission, not ours.

Unless someone ahead of us was in trouble, he shouldn't be asking, and I begged off hesitatingly. I wanted free of this command business. I wanted to hide.

The pilot gave an order.

I toweled off my face and consulted the map. I had to make a decision. *Me.*

"Tell him to get fucked, Irish," Sergeant Crisco, my likely successor, said. He'd come out of the program at Ft. Benning convinced he knew everything. Worse, he usually did.

The others looked at me in tentative agreement.

"We have to follow," I said.

"We *don't* have to follow," Crisco went on. "He's a warrant officer. He ain't jackshit unless the Colonel says he is."

"Move out!" I said.

"Fucking candy-ass," Crisco muttered.

Hovering sixty feet above us, the pilot followed a trail through bamboo and tall ferns, veering off when Screwy Louie discovered the bunker complex. What if they hit us now? What if there was a company of them, against our fifteen? What if someone died? It would all be because I hadn't stood up to that damned warrant officer.

But, like the village, the bunkers had long been abandoned. Louie pointed us inside the old perimeter and collapsed, letting the others search for documents or rusty weapons. He smiled wearily. "Why we do that, Irish?"

I looked away.

"We out here for a *week,* man. We don't get no soft bed like the flier. We don't get no fucking hot *meal.* They getting to you, man. You *like* this army shit. You a goddamn lifer, Irish?"

"Hey, babes," Detroit said. "Irish, he the short-timer. He just laying low."

"We'll camp here," I said, trying to muster some authority. We moved up the trail another two hundred meters and set up ambushes, a kilometer short of where we had been ordered to be, but our true destination wouldn't look any different than this one. And maybe my troops would stop harassing me.

I called Battalion, faking the coordinates, and Crisco turned away with a smirk.

"You got a problem?"

"Not me, Commander."

Battalion called back, and I drew a deep breath. "This is Bandit 6, go ahead."

"Roger, Bandit 6, new location. Move to Golf one, one, niner, one, one, five."

"Shit," Crisco said. "If you're gonna fake the coordinates, do it later in the day."

I ignored him. "Objective?"

I had to remember it was some Specialist on the other end, for whom we were nothing but pins on a map. "Roger. Objective: Golf one, one, niner, one, one, five."

Five more kilometers—two kilometers further than if we had been where I'd reported we were. And you could bet that the new coordinates pinpointed an identical piece of nowhere. "All right," I said. "Saddle up!"

"John *Wayne*," Louie said.

"*Point!*"

He looked at me as if I'd struck him, but staggered to his feet. How had Sherry handled this so smoothly? He was an officer, I thought, not a substitute. He was also *right*. He wouldn't have faked the coordinates, and, if he had, like Sergeant Crisco, he'd have done so at a smarter time.

The ground dropped to a ravine, choked with vines, that broadened to a mucky depression cluttered with anthills and thorn trees. Louie stopped to wipe sweat from his eyes. He took deep breaths. He bent at the hips, braced one hand on a knee, shifted his pack far forward, and doubled his towel under the straps to take the weight of the pack again.

He backed into a nest of fire ants and we waited while he shook loose his gear and tore off his shirt. He beat frantically at his chest and his face wrenched. "*Jesuchristo!*"

Grimacing, he took a long drink and then stood shivering. If I touched him, I thought, he'd fall over. I wasn't mean enough for this job. "Move it!"

He did, but in fifty meters the file snarled up just short of a clearing. Cross the clearing, and we had reached the coordinates. Why stop?

Every part of me was wet. My sick neck was on fire. My eyes ran down the file and I could have killed them all, each for separate reasons. What use did they have on earth? Who would miss them but their mothers? I stalked forward. "What is it? What the fuck's wrong now?"

"Louie," Jim Cole said quietly. "Stroked out."

He lay in the grass with a towel over his face. His chest and arms quivered.

On the other hand, maybe I *was* mean enough.

I waved an arm for the men to take a break, and they fell to the ground where they were standing. The medic eyed me neutrally, poured water all over Louie, and propped his head on a damp towel. He held salt water to his lips. "We'll have to take him out, Irish."

I stalked ahead, crouched in the high grass, and took a long drink. I leaned against a mammoth bamboo and looked across the clearing toward a B-52 crater. It had been made perhaps six months before. Rocks had flown up all around it and vulcanized, so that nothing grew there, and might never grow. I took another drink.

Jim Cole drew near. "You okay?"

"I'm sick of this, Jim Cole. I want to go home."

"Sure. I got a little daughter I never seen." He spat carefully between his boots. "Don't let Crisco get to you, my friend. He *wants* you to look bad. He wants your job."

"Christ, it's his. I don't know how Ransom did it."

"Never lost his cool."

"One time he did, Jim Cole. On the river?"

"When we made the bridge! And Lieutenant Sherry got killed. That was—"

"The good old days?"

He shrugged. I returned to the file, gave Crisco a big smile, and knelt beside Louie. "Hot day, huh? Damn near passed out myself."

"Fuck, man … "

Detroit tipped up one of Louie's canteens, sloshing the water thoughtfully. Then his face twisted and he spat. "Alka-Seltzer!"

Laughter ran down the file.

"No wonder he stroke out. Louie humping Alka-Seltzer!"

"Got a bad stomach," Jim Cole explained.

"You kick my feet, man," Louie muttered. "Don't kick my feet!"

Kick his feet? Why would I want to kick his feet? "What, Louie?"

"Feet!"

"Just rest," I said. I couldn't tell if he understood me. "Nobody's gonna kick your feet. Hot meal tonight. Soft bed. Yvette Mimieux comes to you—"

"In your dreams!" Crisco said, but he was grinning.

"—and slowly undresses."

"Mmmm," Louie said.

I dropped into the elephant grass again, sitting on my helmet to await the dustoff. I dumped a canteen full of Alka-Seltzer water onto my head and closed my eyes. One thing at a time, I thought. Norman had it worse.

As if nothing were more natural, four North Vietnamese walked out of the woodline directly across from me. It seemed *so* natural that I might have stepped into the clearing and greeted them. *Go away,* I would have told them, in my weariness. *I have no interest in you, go away.*

They looked left and right. They talked low, their words hardly carrying. Their point man looked straight at me, but I was motionless in the grass. His eyes kept traveling.

I turned and whispered. "Call it off. Call off the bird!"

"What?"

"We got contact. Tell 'em to shut up back there!"

Three of the soldiers dropped from sight, over the berm of the crater. I heard their laughter, and splashes as they jumped in. A swim. Yes, how wonderful.

The point man squatted on the berm with his AK-47, but he was a poor guard. He stood and pulled off his shirt, too, but the two in the water yelled for him to stay put. I remembered Ransom, catching me in Dietrich's pool. *Can't have no minutes, Irish.*

Crisco crawled beside me. "Irish, what the—?"

"Shut up! We got 'em. You see? We *got* 'em."

"Motherfuck, Irish."

They could not have positioned themselves more to our advantage. I motioned for the men to come on line as if for an assault, then brought a finger to my lips. Jim Cole and Detroit crawled near with the gun. I shook my head.

Crisco looked at me fearfully. "You—"

"Shoot him."

"*Shoot* him?"

"They can't get out of the water. Prisoners! But we have to get *him.*"

Crisco and I lay side by side, steadied our rifles, aimed for the little man's heart. I was sweating. My neck ached. The air seemed to thunder around me, and, for an instant, the soldier blurred in waves of heat. I focused, squeezed the trigger, relented. Let him go. What did I care if he lived or died?

Crisco looked at me. I sighted once again, and gave the order. "Fire!"

Late in the afternoon, as dust from Chinooks reddened the sky, we hung parachutes between the CQs of Bravo and Charley Companies, and dragged up tables.

Capturing two naked VC, one of them an officer, called for a celebration. Colonel Drake, Captain Bell, and First Sergeant Hickman had pooled their resources to fill the bed of a three-quarter-ton pickup with watermelon, Black Label, and ice. The cook flipped steaks over charcoal. There were potato chips, a twenty-pound chunk of Wisconsin cheddar, and olives. There was ice cream with black walnuts for topping.

Colonel Drake waylaid a band that had been playing at the Filipino officers club, three Vietnamese who spent the afternoon eating watermelon and stringing wires to their cinder block stand. Their lead singer, a girl with hair to her knees who wore a tight, sequined miniskirt such as Ann-Margret was rumored to, arrived near nightfall. She climbed onto the stand, grabbed the microphone, and said, "One, two... *tasting.*" The drummer did a theatrical roll and tossed his sticks in the air, the lead guitar struck some Hendrix chords, and the band settled in with Beatles tunes.

They were flat as an open soda. The girl's voice was piercingly high, a wail amid the wailing guitars. Still, I was amazed at the imitation, and lay on a table with my head against a rucksack, growing used to the fact that I was a hero.

In fact, I had command potential. They'd write of my exploits, and teach my strategies at West Point. I sang along with the girl, imagining who'd play me in the movies, as the night spun deliriously beneath the fluttering silk, in the darting, streaked light the diesel candles threw.

Detroit dipped his head to Jim Cole and they rose to dance, not exactly with each other. Others stood by themselves, shuffling with the beat, drinking. The drummer grinned and the girl did a shimmy, her hands plunging high.

Colonel Drake walked by, waving grandly. "Carry on, carry on," he called, and ducked into company headquarters. He emerged with Captain Bell—slapped some shoulders, took a swallow of beer, and left.

Bell grabbed a beer and circulated, trying to look relaxed, but eying the girl warily. He worked his way determinedly to my side, stepping over men sprawled in the dust. He shook my hand. "Colonel Drake is very pleased. A citation, I think."

"Thank you, sir."

"I'm putting *you* in for a Bronze Star."

"The men, sir. I didn't do anything."

"I know what you did." He stared across the greenline as the band struck up "Suzy Q" and everyone began dancing in earnest. "You should consider reenlisting, Irish."

I didn't answer for a moment. "Yessir."

"Well!" He laughed. "I'll put you in for a leave, then. Taipei? Bet you'd like *that.*"

"Yessir!"

He went off to join Drake. I put up my feet and watched Crisco bounce and whirl: he did a cartwheel and sprung to the stand, where he put his arm around the girl. She wasn't impressed. She kept singing, but shook her head angrily. Crisco turned, bent back at the waist like a bronc rider, and pantomimed jacking off.

Good-bye, young sergeant, I thought.

Hickman appeared with a projector and reels of film.

"What's *that?*"

"Entertainment first class, soldier! Irish, you thread this?"

He sat heavily, watching me work. "Irish, I have something to say. I thought you was the o-riginal fuckup for the longest time. But I think, I truly and honestly think, you ought to—"

"I've considered it, First Sergeant."

"I can get you … another promotion. Staff sergeant? Bonus! Irish, manjack smart as you could be a warrant officer. Or maybe go to OCS!" He dropped his eyes. "Wouldn't have to stay infantry."

I finished threading the projector. "Thank you, First Sergeant."

He ran a hand over his skull. "Wrong time to be in the army, hell, I know that. Ain't the army's fault. Army's just the army, Irish!" He looked up mournfully. "Been good to *me.*"

"When do you retire?"

"I leave next week. And I got to do three months at Carson."

"Then?"

But whatever he said was gobbled up in the movie's soundtrack and the screams from the men. The band couldn't see the screen, but they could see the men's faces. They had been playing "One Hundred Miles," but cranked it down as if someone had pulled a plug.

Screwy Louie stumbled downhill from the barracks, having slept around the clock. He grabbed a slice of watermelon and plopped in the dirt before the screen.

"First Sergeant?"

"Yes, Sergeant Donnelly."

"You hear anything about Norman?"

Off on the greenline a fire mission began: *Boom!... Boom!...
Boom!*

The old man's eyes bulged as he concentrated on the movie.
"No, Irish. Man in the stockade, you never do."

As the woman stepped from her shower, the doorbell rang,
and she threw a towel around her and hurried through the parlor.
It was a vacuum cleaner salesman. He dropped his trousers immediately, revealing polka-dot shorts, and ran after the woman with
his sweeper, accompanied by the band's last attempt at "One Hundred Miles," and deafening cheers. Quickly enough, the woman
lay writhing on her bed.

The drummer stopped, plainly disgusted, and turned to
pack his equipment. He came down from the stand and watched,
too, as the salesman fucked the woman. One guitar still wailed,
and the girl sang a line or two of her finale, "San Francisco."

She stared at me, her only audience, and stopped. She
marched uphill a few feet, puffing angrily on a cigarette exactly as
Trudy used to. She looked at me imploringly, as if I could do something to salvage her gig, and I almost went after her. She would
have thought I wanted sex, and perhaps I did. I was too drunk to
know. I lay back on the table and the stars hurtled by.

Ten days later I dropped in my nickel at the airfield in Ton Son
Nhut and flew to Taipei. It was my reward for heroism. Taipei was
a sort of soldiers' theme park, and I doubt if you could have
escaped its attractions if you tried.

"Shari" was my age, and had been a prostitute for three
years. I wasn't quite a person for her, but merely another big,
meaty, male Caucasian—male, principally, not significantly different
from the several hundred who had preceded me.

For my part, I kept confusing her with the Vietnamese singer
and even with Cuc Hoa, but we didn't need to regard each other
with precision. Do emergency workers become involved with all
their overdoses, their broken children, their heart failures?
Absolutely not. Shari and I were soldiers, prepared to forget each
other immediately.

"You have bad neck."

"It won't go away. I've tried—"

"No sweat."

She insisted on being on top. I could place my thumbs at her bony waist, my fingers over her buttocks, and lift her up and down—a move not unlike a bench press. Her tiny breasts flopped and her stomach ran with sweat. In the dark I tried to imagine she was Trudy. But after a while it was as though she weren't there, as if I were copulating with air.

I found television more interesting. Americans had landed on the moon, and the astronauts cruised in their electric dune buggy. It was *his*tory, Norman.

"True?" Shari asked.

"You mean is it a show? No, of course it's true."

Shari hunched down in her chair, kicked off her sandals, and crossed her legs, jerking one of them nervously. She lit a cigarette. She glanced around the dim lobby, then reached beneath her skirt and peeled off her stockings. She crossed to the sofa, curled next to me, and put my hand between her legs. "I make you happy?"

I took back my hand. "Sure."

"Then why you not give me money?"

"I gave you money."

"Other soldiers, they give girls *all* their money. Then, girl take *care* of soldier."

"I see." I reached into my billfold and gave her everything but a fifty. "All yours," I said.

She disappeared. Good money after bad, I thought, but I didn't care. I slumped in the chair, studied the universe, and speculated on what fifty dollars would buy.

Shari returned with two bottles of beer and a platter of fried prawns. The prawns were gigantic, tender, wonderful. The beer had a tang of ginger. She settled near me and we watched Neil Armstrong leap across the dusty horizon.

"Okay, we stay here," she said. "Watch TV. Just like America."

I woke that night gently, with the sensation of falling like a feather falls, or like a man drifts down to the moon; Shari was rubbing a salve along my neck. I jerked in alarm, but she said, "No, no, good for you."

I didn't believe it. I hardly thought about it at all. But two days later, when Shari had ceased to exist, I sat waiting for a C-130 to taxi around and fly me to Sông Trì, rubbing my smooth neck.

Before my leave Hickman handed me two letters from Cindy, and I sat on the same bench where Sims and I had sat on his way to LBJ, turning the letters over in my hands, but not opening them. I opened them now, seven days later.

Cindy wrote about married student housing and about how I could finish my education with the G.I. Bill. She said she loved me. I felt trapped, thinking I'd written all those things to Cindy because I was desperate and sad, and thinking, as kind as she'd been, that I could not fail to go to her. I thought of Shari, a Chinese prostitute who had healed me for a price, and, at that moment, loved her more than Cindy.

Maybe that's the secret of love: you get what you pay for.

13

Into the Sunset

I COULD HARDLY sleep through the long flight. It was three in the morning, it took an hour to find a taxi, and I felt as though I were on point without a weapon. Oakland in 1969. I can't recommend it.

I called Dad from San Francisco: no answer. Where else could I go? To Cindy, but the prospect frightened me, suddenly.

I tried calling Dad again at midday, from Denver. He didn't answer at dusk in Kansas City, and then it was nine in the evening and I was walking the square in unfamiliar Springfield, so weary I could hardly get out the words to ask directions. Ten blocks to his rental house—my home, in a manner of speaking, though I'd never been there.

Saturday night, I realized, walking past a tavern. Men shouted and women laughed, not understanding that they had to be silent, that they could be ambushed any instant.

The door was unlocked. "Hello?" I said. "Daddy?" I dropped my duffel bag onto the sagging porch and stalked into the kitchen. I thought, this isn't his house at all, but no, there was that old photograph of my great-grandfather's orchard in Maryland, and now the Kelvinator, Mom's Kelvinator from the country, that she defrosted every week, came on with the same squawk as always.

I'm the same, I thought. I'm all right.

Except that my mother was dead and the farm, a poor farm but with a big woods to wander in, and a pond for catching catfish, was gone.

I turned on the TV, also from our old house, and saw a formation of helicopters. There was a shot of a grunt lieutenant with weary troops behind him, and I looked for Norman's face, and Worm's, and Sherry's. I felt dizzy, and sat quickly on the couch. I couldn't control my arms, and they danced about as if I'd lost motor function. My face in the mirror opposite wasn't mine at all. The man I saw there was crying.

I opened the Kelvinator and couldn't make sense of the contents, but grabbed a chunk of cheese and staggered into what I surmised to be the guest room. I fell asleep, sobbing.

I woke to a gust of wind rattling the window. It was dark, hot, and for an instant I thought I was in Sông Trì.

Mom's cuckoo clock hissed and scolded. A light went on in the kitchen and I whispered, "Mommy," and thought, supper will be soon. Lying there, I could have stood and taken my place on guard, or gone out to play with the neighbor girl. Then I thought, *Daddy,* and tried to say the word. Oh, Daddy, it's Jimmy. I was lost in the woods but I'm home now.

A woman crossed the doorway toward the stove and returned with a saucepan. She sat at the table, reading from a paperback romance, eating out of the saucepan. She kicked off her shoes, and, with a sudden gesture, hunched up in the chair to pull down her stockings.

I lay contemplating her bare legs, hoping she'd turn so I could see more, because, if this was Dad's girlfriend, he'd done all right. Then I was afraid. Which was better: to turn over, pretend to sleep, and let her discover me, or to march in and say hello?

I slipped across the hall and stood in the doorway. "Ma'am—"

She dropped the saucepan to the floor, scattering ringlets of spaghetti. The spaghetti slopped by my shoes, and I couldn't concentrate, even as she scooted back, tipped over in her chair, caught herself with a hand. Her black eyes were angry, frightened, and she tensed as though about to leap to the sink for a knife.

"Hey! I'm Irish—I mean Jim, Jimmy. Patrick. Whatever you want to call me! I'm—"

"I know, I know—oh. You never called!"

"I did. Yes, ma'am, I sure tried to."

Her breasts heaved and she held a hand to her heart. "You really scared me. I worked late today, I wasn't here." She forced a smile. "Welcome home, Jim!"

"Patrick."

"Patrick, your father is in New Jersey. On a run."

"You're—"

"Mavis. Your father's—well, we're engaged. I don't live here—I wouldn't, I wouldn't *live* with a man. George and I are planning to get married this winter. This house—*your* house, Patrick—it's close to work, and sometimes I ..."

It was plain enough that she'd moved in with the old man, but that she hadn't planned on delivering the news herself. Nor on hosting his grown son.

"I'll just sit here and have a cigarette." I held her lighter and she lit a Marlboro, meeting my eyes as she released smoke. "It's not a good witness for the Lord, is it? But I don't smoke, not really. I get nervous. You put a scare in me." She smashed the cigarette and lit another. "So what are your plans, Patrick?"

I fell into the chair across from her. "Go back to college, I guess."

She put her hand on my arm and looked up at me. "I'm sorry you had to go through all that."

I grasped her hand until she yanked it back. "So how did you and my dad get together?"

"He'd come to the Kanoke, that's where I work, real early for breakfast. Five o'clock, even before the farmers are out. He'd drink three cups of coffee and just sit there, staring, like he was trying to work up his nerve to get in that truck again."

"I don't know him like this," I said. "I remember him from the drought—everything going wrong. We lost the place. Mom died. I went off to school—we didn't get along so well."

She drew in a breath. She was a handsome woman, middle-aged, but a lot younger than Dad. "He took your mother's death real hard. I could see it on his face, he was hurting so bad. But I knew he liked me, so I started talking to him."

"Did he ever mention me?"

"He said you were in combat, Patrick, and he hoped you didn't get wounded."

I reached for Mavis's cigarettes. A Bible-thumper, but she smoked. It confounded my view of the world. "Vietnam was real fucked up."

She blinked. "This is your home, Patrick, I want you to think of this as your home, but I would appreciate it if you restrained your language."

"It was *bad*. Nobody knew why we were there." I stared, and for an instant couldn't control myself, her bare legs crossing and uncrossing in my head. I wanted to lean over and kiss her, and pull her close so that her breasts mashed into me, and stroke her face. She saw it in my eyes and turned her head. And I thought, what in the world is wrong with me?

"This chaplain," I said, grasping for words. "This is an awful thing, Mavis."

"Go ahead."

"Some hippy came up and spit on him there in Oakland. A chaplain." I stared at her meaningfully. I almost believed the story, but I'd heard it somewhere. The only chaplain I knew had banished a young woman to prostitution, and her lover to jail. "A *chaplain*."

"That's a terrible thing for anybody to see," she said. Sympathy crept into her eyes, and forgiveness for my strange lust. "You're home now, Patrick. You have your whole life ahead of you."

"You got a car? Let's go get some ice cream."

She seemed puzzled. "I'm worn out. I'm not fixed up."

"You look fine." I grinned. "The old man did good."

She dug in her purse for keys, hands trembling. "You go. I think Metzger's is open."

*   *   *

It's a sharp memory, still: driving Mavis's Ford through the warm night, pulling up at the DQ where the long-legged high school girls flirted with every male who looked their way—except for me. I frightened them.

There was a woman walking the square and I taxied behind her for a while, until she turned, terrified, and I sped away, wondering what sort of monster she saw.

I bought a six-pack of beer and sat on the college grounds, but I couldn't connect with anything. The students were my age and yet were babies, babbling, full of nonsense.

I came in at midnight and fell on the bed, drunk, ironic, confused. Mavis stood in the doorway in her housecoat, hair mussed from sleep. "I was worried about you. You're not, you're not—"

"I took a little drive, that's all. There's some ice cream in the refrigerator."

She padded off and returned with a dish of rocky road. "I shouldn't eat this," she said. "I don't need the calories."

I rolled over and stared up at her. "Oh, you're a good-looking woman, Mavis."

"Anything would look good to you."

I laughed. "Come sit with me."

"I cain't."

"Pretty, pretty please. I get bad dreams." I wiggled under the covers. "Come tuck me in!"

Frowning, she pulled the bedclothes up and slid a pillow under my head. "Whoo," she said. "You smell like a still."

"Good night, Mommy," I said, and she laughed and I knew she couldn't resist me. I grabbed her arm and pulled her to the bed. She managed to twist a little so that she sat upright, rather than falling beside me, but I slipped a hand inside her housecoat and found a breast.

"Patrick, no, no, you're drunk."

"Please?"

"No!" she said, and yanked from me, ran from the room. A door slammed. A lock engaged, and I thought, where am I? Mommy, Daddy, where did you go?

*   *   *

The old man came in late the next evening. To my mind he was still a farmer, not a truck driver, and I couldn't get used to his talk. He worked for a national freight company, and made good money, he said. The rundown house was temporary. He was going to build a fine new one when Mavis and he got married. I should come and visit him then, though I was welcome anytime, of course.

Mavis and I had made it through the day, mostly by avoiding each other. I took a long walk, and bought some magazines on the square, and saw a movie. Not so bad, I thought: no wounds, money in my pockets, education paid for.

Complaining of a headache, Mavis slipped away after supper, and the old man and I sat in the living room. I'd tuned the television to a Cardinals game, having forgotten that he hated sports. When I was a kid he'd storm into the house and stomp upstairs, where I was attempting to watch the World Series. "We got work to do!"

Remembering, I turned the game off and tried to listen to him. There was that odd sense of losing control again. Pure rage boiled up in me, not directed at him exactly, but present like bad food in my stomach, like a headache. I didn't hear all that he said, but I knew he hadn't asked one question about Vietnam.

"Mavis is an awful nice woman," he said.

"She is."

"I was worried about being older, but after a while it didn't seem to matter. She loves me for what I am. She rescued me. Even talked me into going to church again."

"Again? I don't ever remember you going."

"When your mother passed on—"

I made a big sigh, and there was that bucket of anger again. It was a thing apart, something I could cut out of me, perhaps, and throw to the dogs. "Can we not talk about my mother? Please?"

He cleared his throat. "I said, 'Mavis, I got this house. It's not so fine, I wouldn't pretend it is, but it's paid for.' And I'll fix it up, I told her. I put in that washer and dryer, and then she wanted a dishwasher. I tell you, Jimmy, a man goes to a lot of trouble for a woman."

"I like to be called Patrick," I said.

"Of course, she ought to have a dishwasher if she wants one, but women don't understand. You'll find out, one of these days."

One of his few prophetic utterances.

"I had to put in a bigger water heater, and run all new copper in there under the sink, on account of the black pipe was so full of crud. Then you got to keep your temperature hotter even though you only use your dishwasher every couple days. Here I am on the road two weeks, sometimes, and it runs the bill up for nothing. I reckon that's what a man does for love."

"You never wrote me," I said. "Not once."

"Aw, I meant to, Jimmy."

"Nobody wrote me." Which, of course, wasn't true, since Cindy had. "Not even a fucking Christmas card."

"You watch your language in this house."

"A *mother*fucking card."

"Mavis won't stand for it, I'll tell you that."

I rose and walked to the window. I slapped my head as if I could jostle its contents until they made sense. I hated myself. I'd tried to seduce my stepmother. "I'm sorry," I said, peering through the curtains. If I hit the road yet tonight, where could I go? "I'm so sorry." To Cindy. I could make it there by dawn.

"You don't want me to talk about your mother, but she was my wife and she was precious to me. Right there on her deathbed, you know well as I do it was her last wish, I turned over my life to Jesus. You're welcome here, Jimmy. You get out of the service and wanta stay here awhile, that's fine. I *want* you to."

"Oh, shut up," I said, wheeling.

It was as if I'd struck him. Good, I thought.

"There you was, Jimmy, almost grown." He was whining now. "And then you was gone, I didn't have nobody."

"You're just living with her, aren't you? You ain't gonna bother to get married."

"That's not true. I think—I think it's been a long day. Everybody's tired. I think—I think you're full of trouble because of the bad experiences you've had. I know I coulda done better, but I was thinking about you, and you know, take an aching heart to the Lord, Jimmy. We'll be praying for you—"

"You got her bought and paid for with your goddamn dishwasher. You just want something to fuck."

"Son—!"

I stumbled into the kitchen. The lights flickered, and then I understood that it was me, that I was going to black out. I clung to the wall and fumbled my way down the hall for my gear, and there was Mavis by the bathroom door, eyes blazing.

Dad had come from the living room. "You sit right down here, Mister. This is my house, I don't care where you been. Who you think you are?"

"Nobody," I said, pivoting on heel, and then I set out to spend a lifetime proving it.

Why visit with such memories, now that he's dead? Can I be excused because I had just returned from Vietnam?

Through those first weeks I kept testing myself in crowds, looking about to see if people sensed the killer among them, the man who had seen dead bodies piled high as the moon. I thought, will it from your mind. Pretend there was no Norman, no Dranow, no helicopter in the feeble light of dawn.

Cindy and I were married before the summer was out. My anger wasn't hard and discrete as a boil on the neck then, but spread through my bloodstream. Quickly, I learned to pass for normal. Maybe I *was* normal.

While I always knew where Dad was, he and I never reconciled. "You should visit your father," Cindy would say, and I knew she was right, but didn't go.

The four of us did see each other occasionally, and Mavis and Cindy got along well enough, but the best the old man and I could manage was prolonged silence. In the end, it's hard for me to say why. He was a rough father, but not unusually cruel. My mother had a hard life, but not because he mistreated her. I couldn't fathom it for years, but as I grow older I believe the trouble was that I looked at him and saw myself.

Toward the end he asked me to come down. There was a mysterious tone in his voice and I had my guard up, though I stopped off at a flea market to buy him some westerns as a peace offering. We took a drive in his beautiful Studebaker, and he labored hard for positive things to say about me—a chore with which I myself would have had difficulty.

Then, like the old days, we began to argue. Mavis intervened, and when she and I came out from the grocery he'd had his heart attack. Next thing I knew Mavis and I sat beside him in the hospital. His eyes were open but expressionless.

"Brought you some books, Dad," I said, holding up the westerns. Grim, lonely men on crusades, riding off into the sunset. There was even one by his favorite, Ernest Haycox.

He hadn't spoken all day, but surprised us both by muttering something now. "Shoney's," he whispered.

"He wants to go to Shoney's!" Mavis said. "Honey, you get better now, we'll go to Shoney's. Yes, we will!"

Not at all, I thought. "Shawnee," I said, knowing he'd recognized one of the westerns. "They killed his family. They took his land." Which was not so far from his obituary—if obituaries were ever so truthful.

"Huh," Dad said. "Whiman."

White man. He hated blacks but romanticized the Indians. "Yes, the white man did it. So he started walking, the—the Shawnee, walking west. Living off the land." What did Indians do, at least in westerns? "He wasted nothing, he needed no one, he … he was walking. And he came to—to a beautiful valley. Dad?"

He'd closed his eyes, and I really thought he was dying. But he squeezed my hand, and I went on, thinking maybe he deserved a beautiful valley if only for his survival skills.

"Down between the mountains. There were tall pine trees whistling in the wind, and fields of yellow and purple flowers, and

a wonderful trout stream. Really clear, Dad. Full of those fat rain-
bows. And the Shawnee met a beautiful maiden there, from a tribe
that lived in the valley, a tribe that had never known war."

I spun it out awhile longer, and maybe he heard, and liked
the story. You never know. He died late that evening, and whether
or not I had helped him I had at least helped Mavis, and made up
for the ancient offense she'd long since forgiven me for.

"It was the most beautiful story I ever heard," she said. She
retold it a dozen times at the funeral, and incorporated it into her
personal vision of heaven. She came to see us for several years
afterwards, and her eyes softened when she looked at me.

So many of the deaths I've known have been remote, occur-
ring long after love has crashed or I've betrayed my best instincts.
I held Worm in my arms and could not help, I couldn't help
Norman, and maybe I didn't help my father. But *there I was,* Dad,
and I gave it a try.

14

The Bravest Man in Warner, Oklahoma

THE OLD C-130 jolted about so much that I didn't realize we had landed. The gate cranked down and light streamed in. I dropped to the red earth, and it was as though I were coming in to Sông Trì for the first time, rather than the last. It was just as wild, just as mammoth and confusing.

How terrible, that such a place was more like home than Missouri.

There was no one in the barracks. I walked to my bunk but the mattress was turned up, the blankets gone. Of course! *I* had done that, because the company had headed to the field just as I was bound for Taiwan.

The mess hall was closed tight. I knocked on the door but no one answered.

I walked to company headquarters, where a typewriter beat like a drum. "Hello?"

"Who are you?"

Who are *you?* I wondered. He had bushy black hair and, though he was smooth-shaven, his beard was so heavy it darkened his face. He settled in his chair and lit a cigarette.

"My name's James Patrick Donnelly," I said, smiling, holding out a hand. I didn't feel friendly but, at the moment, this man mattered more than anyone in the world. "Maybe you have my orders? I know Hickman's gone now, but he must have—"

"Irish. Yes, I've heard about you." He looked down at his typewriter keys as if our conversation had concluded.

Cheerfully, I would have shot him. "Seems like my orders should be done, Specialist. Waiting for me right here on your desk."

He blew a cloud of smoke. "Can't do a *thing* without Lieutenant Dailey says so."

"Ah. New lieutenant." It wouldn't do any good to kill him, I thought. Another would grow in his place. "So where's he?"

The specialist sighed, as if it were a trial simply to speak. "They're all down on the pad, the whole battalion. You didn't see them? Hot poop, young sergeant. They think they've found that VC headquarters you guys missed."

"So I find Dailey—"

"Here." The clerk opened a file drawer and drew out some blank forms. "Captain Bell's in Hawaii with his wife. Dailey's the XO: he signs these, I'll fill 'em in. You have to check out with the AID station, turn in your gear—I don't think you can do all that today."

"Thanks," I said. "I'll try."

Alpha, Bravo, and Charley were lined up platoon by platoon, but not really in formation. Some men milled about and some sat on the strip, hunched against their gear, backs to the wind. Dust filled the air, and the strip was hot enough to melt boot soles. I stopped to drench my towel in a bucket of rainwater, then wrapped it around my face.

I couldn't spot my own platoon, though I saw the man who must be Dailey; he was the only lieutenant I didn't recognize.

"Sir, my name is James Donnelly. I see you're busy, sir, but I—"

"Irish! Heard so much about you! Sergeant Crisco says you're the best we got!"

"Crisco?" My eyes fled toward the men. And now I saw Detroit, waving at me. I grinned and waved back.

"Absolutely, Irish! Captured three prisoners? Why you think we're all standing out here in the heat, anyhow? It's *your* information! Your *chieu hois* talked!"

I stepped back. "You're shitting me."

"Great timing, Irish!"

Then again, maybe not.

Dailey's tone grew confidential. "Last night we confirmed it. This air force shithook took a fifty-one through the forward rotor. Ordnance like that, I don't have to tell you—"

"Yessir." I held my release forms in the wind. "I'm trying to—"

"Later, later," the Lieutenant hissed, motioning with the back of his hand, and drawing himself to attention. "Ten-hut!" someone cried out, and, all down the line, soldiers stirred and stood erect. I dropped clumsily into the ranks beside Detroit.

"At *ease*," the Colonel said, and four hundred men put their arms behind their backs. "Sweet Jesus, men! We found it! You gonna go out there tonight, and dig in deep, and if old Charley comes out of the bushes, his shit is weak. His shit is weaker than gook tea, men!"

"Where's Screwy Louie?" I whispered.

Detroit smiled. "Went to Manila. Man's *way* overdue."

I was the one who'd put him in for a leave. "Jim Cole?"

"He dead, Irish. Jim Cole dead."

The Colonel pointed at soldiers up and down the line. "I don't care what they say on TV. I don't care what the people back home say, these protesters. That bitch, Jane Fonda? The American soldier is the fightingest soldier the world has ever known! We are gonna kick ass, men! We are gonna bring Charley down to a little bloody smear!"

Detroit stared straight ahead. "He set off a trip-flare and Lonely blew him away."

"*We* killed him?"

"Fuckin' new guys."

The Colonel at last was done. There were more salutes, more shouts, and a great rustling of bodies and equipment as, behind us, the helicopters throttled up.

Detroit shouldered his pack. "What you *do*ing here, my man?"

Crisco ran up near, nodding. "That's right, get outta here, Irish. War's over for you."

I paused, thinking what an inadequate way to say good-bye it was, but I had already said good-bye, and wasn't supposed to be there at all. Detroit shook my hand. "See you in the World, brother," he said, and I slapped his shoulder awkwardly, and ran after Dailey. He was hurrying back and forth to organize his platoon—*my* platoon—and set them trotting toward the pad.

"Sir! All you have to do—"

"Borrow First Sergeant's rifle, Irish. I'll sign those papers tonight. Move!"

I almost didn't. I almost laughed in his face. What could he do, send me to Vietnam?

Hell, I could go to the Colonel for *his* signature. He and I were buddies.

Then, as my eyes glanced over Bravo Company, I saw Sims.

His hair was shaven close, like a marine recruit's. He'd lost weight. His skin was ashen.

His platoon had grouped in earnest and was boarding the first lift. He drew even closer, as his bird hovered in a turn, and I waved frantically. His eyes crossed mine, traveled onward, whipped backward. He grinned. "I-rish," his lips said, and he threw me his silly salute.

We came down at dark on the high side of a field of tall grass, while Bravo Company landed on the low side and threaded into the mangroves. As we were landing I saw the destroyers a few miles away, on the South China Sea.

We made camp. I tried to help but no one would let me work. All through the evening men crept up to say good-bye, to offer choice delicacies from the Care packages their mothers and aunts and girlfriends had sent. I volunteered for guard with the gun team, but Detroit laughed.

"You the King. We treat you right."

"Why is Norman in Bravo?" I asked him.

"Dailey didn't want him. He a troublemaker, Irish, that's what they say."

But it was also that Dranow *had* wanted him. After their charge on that abandoned woods he thought of him as a fearless, kindred spirit. Here was a man who had received the Silver Star. All Sims needed was better discipline, and Dranow, if he had nothing else worth mentioning, had discipline.

I crawled from the hooch and lay on the open ground. A mellow light bathed the trees, and I looked up at that slice of moon. I wondered how it was that I could be here, and astronauts could be there. "Detroit," I whispered. "You know what the Southern Cross is?"

"Have to do with boxing," he said.

"No, no, it's—"

But he was grinning, and lifting his arm. "Just look at the Milky Way."

And there it was, low on the horizon but as stunningly bright, and obvious, as advertised. "Amazing," I said. "I looked for that all year."

"Shoulda ast me," Detroit said.

Around three, the firing began. I woke again, jumped in the hole, but in an instant knew that it wasn't meant for us. Across the grass, down in the swamp, Bravo Company was getting mauled.

The firing went on much too long, and, after a while, most of it was the popcorn sound of AK-47s, or the *doop! doop! doop!* of mortars. I kept listening for our machine guns, but they never began. Flares swished and made a wobbly trajectory up, then rained their eerie light. Two Phantoms struck with five-hundred pounders and, as the sun rose, it was quiet. Orders came to link up.

The jungle was dewy and cool, with the sunlight cascading through the triple canopy. We marched silently and there weren't any birds, only the occasional lizard squawking her insults. The point man halted at a burned-out area.

There was a plain, perhaps a square mile of burned-off grass, where shells had gone wide and a fire raged. The ground smoked. Here and there trees had caught the silks of falling flares, and these rustled quietly in the wind, the flags of no-man's-land.

Dailey came up and looked out neutrally. He shook his head and pointed straight across. We broke into two columns, and quick-marched. Was the enemy still there, even one, a judicious sniper? The Lieutenant didn't think so, but I wasn't frightened, in any case. My time of danger had passed.

We descended into the swamp, threading through mangrove roots that lifted up like open mouths, and the stench of methane rose. The ground was soft, a slop beneath our boots. We left the mangroves, waded salt water, and the jungle closed in. The point man hacked his way through.

Finally, we saw him, one haggard soldier, Bravo's outpost. He motioned slightly with his head but didn't speak. As we passed he reeled back, his rifle moving, too, like part of his body. I could tell he hadn't slept.

We joined their perimeter. "Hey, man," I heard all around, as soldiers from my company recognized their friends, but no one in Bravo answered. Men stood wrapped in poncho liners, like patients waiting for their beds to be made.

"Norman?" I murmured.

I dropped my gear under a tall orange tree. High above, where the sun's rays broke feebly through, I saw the small fruits, and here were orange smears in the mud where men had stepped. I saw the oranges and, for a moment, didn't see *them*, wrapped in green: the long line of dead.

In the center were the walking wounded, hanging on until we could get them to the sea, and then to the rear. Dranow, haggard and half-asleep, was among them.

One man couldn't wait. I heard the distant throbbing of the Medevac. "Roger. Doc on board," blared the radio. The Bravo medics, with the last of their strength, had slashed a hole in the vines and bamboo, so that they could see the sky. Our own medics rushed forward to help, but halted sharply; it was like intruding upon a wake.

They lashed the man into the litter; his head rolled from side to side, with eyes open, still. The Medevac churned overhead and someone popped a smoke. I can still smell it, like burnt gunpowder and rotten eggs, and see the color: violet.

"That Norman," Detroit said.

Yes. Deep in the night, under flare-light, Dranow had tried an assault, but no one followed. "Alpha Team, move out!" he screamed, and charged for the VC, but he was all the Alpha Team there was. When he had run fifty meters machine gun fire sliced through his legs. He lay bellowing in the night.

Immediately, Sims rose and ran forward. The flare-light died and so, under the waning moon, he made a poor target. He reached Dranow's side, hoisted him in a fireman's carry, ran staggering back. He made it!

But a squad of VC had formed in a reprise of Dranow's efforts, and then they charged. Bravo rallied and cut them down, but one man ran far enough to throw a grenade.

It landed in Sims's squad.

Some men would have watched it explode. Some men would think: *It won't happen, I cannot die.* Sims picked the grenade up, ran five steps, and threw it back.

Not heroism, in a way. Logical. Except, sometimes, those ChiCom grenades were so ancient they didn't explode. Or, if one did, Sims could have hit the ground and, probably, gone uninjured.

The grenade didn't arc three feet before exploding. Sims's stomach and groin were a mass of little holes.

The helicopter drew in at tree level and I could see the medics or doctors or whoever they were, see their faces start in panic as the gunfire broke out again. We opened up on the jungle, Charley and the remnants of Bravo, but where were they?

Sims had gone up and was turning around and around in the litter, his bare feet dangling. The Bravo medics leaped, as though they could help, reach him, push him up.

Why didn't I take care of him, as Lieutenant Sherry asked? If I had talked to the chaplain, long ago! Rather than going to Taiwan, what if I had visited him in jail, and returned to argue his cause? Oh, I wanted to talk to him, pull him through somehow, tell him that in a little while he'd go home. Go home a hero, Norman, the bravest man in Warner, Oklahoma.

The helicopter rose a little; was it taking fire? I couldn't tell in the roar we made. There was a lull, and then *their* fire swept up again. We returned it with everything we had, but something was wrong. The medics had lashed Sims in too quickly, or the helicopter had to pull away to save itself; I never knew.

The men above were leaning down, reaching. But when Sims hit the sky he jerked loose, and the cable crackled in the air and he went tumbling over and over like a yo-yo, and, surely, was dead when he hit the trees.

The Medevac drew away, and the medics dropped to the ground, and the firing ceased.

15

Little Motel on the Prairie

I BOUGHT TWENTY-SEVEN acres east of Carthage. My place, which was once a kind of truck stop, borders a piece of U.S. Route 66, the famous highway that was abandoned with the construction of Interstate 44 twelve miles south. There are a dozen rock cabins in various states of repair, remaining from the days when there was a motel here, too.

Eventually, I will hire a bulldozer to knock the buildings down and carry the debris to a ravine. I have been fixing the fences. Most of the ground is in timber or too sandy for farming, but there are four acres of low ground which would raise corn if I wanted to run a few Angus.

Carthage, like many small towns these days, is a study of lowest common denominators: ignorance, poverty, bland patriotism. There is also a hopeful element to the city, young, rather conservative professional folk who work in Joplin. There's religion, of course. And fishing. The two sports vie for primacy.

I live in the filling station that went with the motel. I have a refrigerator and kitchen range and bed. I have a good well. I grow vegetables and, if it keeps raining, will have a lot of watermelons this year. I've planted apple trees, enough that I might be selling them one day—Jonathans and Winesaps and Arkansas Blacks, but also the New Zealand varieties such as Braeburns and Granny Smiths.

In the winter I heat with wood. I like to sit with my feet propped on the kindling box, sipping mint tea while I grade my eighth graders' papers. I like to sit there, too, and read the *Scientific American* and, on the Internet, call up sites that tell me about Mars. I'm thinking of building a telescope.

I have, as they say, "met someone." Caroline is a counselor at the high school. She's ten years younger than me. She moved here a year ago from Arizona, mostly to escape the man she was living with, a psychic healer. He kept having affairs with women after he cured them of their spiritual debilities.

"We should get together for sex," she said, over the fruit salad at a faculty meeting. "Maybe once a month."

"How about twice?"

"It's a deal."

Caroline's as strange as I am. She wears Navajo jewelry and long, full skirts, and she talks about Buddhism and Native American religions and centering oneself with the earth. She likes to come out on Saturdays and paint landscapes and, sometimes, we take her paintings and leather crafts to shows. I can't make out what she's talking about half the time, but it's nice to have someone to share my tomatoes and sweet corn with, and it's nice to wake up, sometimes, and find there's a woman beside you.

It's more like once a week.

A fair-sized working farm borders me on the north, owned by a hog farmer named Frederickson. I did some carpentry for him in exchange for bush-hogging on my place. He gave me sausages and smoked hams.

Frederickson's older than me and missed the war. When I was in Sông Trì his wife was divorcing him. I think she couldn't stand the smell of pigs. There *is* something worse about pigshit than any of the other varieties.

I suppose you'd call him a hillbilly, though in truth there aren't any hillbillies now, and they were a vanishing species when I was a kid. All the popular assumptions about corncob pipes and half-moons on outhouses and jugs of moonshine were inventions of the movies, it seems to me, though even if they weren't, they're gone now. Still, there are men around who treat their dogs better than their kids, and keep their barns neater than their houses, and insist on doing everything themselves no matter how amateur the result. Frederickson was in that category.

Anyhow, he was alone, too old and odd to find a wife among the local belles. He took to attending church to assuage his loneliness, and someone there gave him one of those listings of Asian women seeking American husbands. "Be nice wife. Like to have good time."

Frederickson flew to Seoul and married a woman half his age who had christened herself Sara Lee. What they had in common was that they were both Baptists.

Sara Lee was better educated than Frederickson but, nonetheless, thought that a farm in Missouri would look like what she had seen on *Dallas*. Frederickson's house had been grand once, no doubt, but was so rundown and bachelorish that when Sara Lee arrived she immediately left again, to live with Korean friends in Tulsa. Perhaps Frederickson hadn't told her he raised pigs.

Of course, he was poor. He'd spent most of his savings flying to Korea. Yet he promised, in trip after trip to Tulsa—on bended knee, more or less—to fix the house. He did, and Sara Lee returned.

They have two children, both of whom speak perfect English. The boy plays baseball. The girl is a prodigy in math. They ride over on their Taiwanese bicycles and play with my son.

Cindy drove down from Jefferson City several weeks ago, bringing Dale for the summer. He's about to be sixteen, and he's anxious for his driver's license.

Cindy's job, as a consumer advocate with the attorney general's office, is going well, though she's looking around for something that pays more. Her husband draws a nice salary but they want to buy a big house overlooking the Missouri River. The three of us drove to Joplin for dinner, and Cindy went on to the Lake of the Ozarks, where her department was on retreat.

Dale doesn't like vegetables except for kohlrabis and sweet corn. I tell him how he used to run barefoot down the corn rows, and I'd catch him at the end pretending to be a monster, but he's far more mature than that now. He wired one of the cabins and plays rock CDs at full volume. Now and then he emerges and hops on my pride and joy, the Kubota L-2500 tractor, and chugs off for the woods.

I have a Springfield rifle of my father's that his father brought home from World War I. On the farm, a rifle is a tool: you lie in wait for that groundhog that's been mowing down your peas. I think, therefore, that Dale should learn about guns.

Used to be my father would shoot a pig on butchering day, and once he made me watch. "Between the eyes, and an inch above," Dad announced. Any other spot, the pig would only be wounded. My father was a good marksman, but this time he did shoot low, and the pig bellowed and staggered crazily around the pen, in bewilderment and rage. I was not partial to killing, in other words, even before I was a soldier.

Still, there are a lot of deer on this place, and I think Dale and I will shoot one this fall, and put up the meat. We'll do it when Caroline isn't around. It would be useless to tell her that the woods are infested with deer and that they menace my apple trees. She's fiercely nonviolent.

You can tell this is worthless ground because it grows black-jack oaks and broom sedge. Toward the back of the place there's another sign of infertility: an outcropping of Osage Orange, also called hedge apples. Dale and I went down there several days ago with the chainsaw, and weaved among the briars to find five straight branches. Osage Orange is a squat, gnarled wood that seldom grows straight.

"What *for*, Dad?" Dale asked, pulling off his headphones for a moment.

"I'm going to make you a bow, and this is the only thing to do it with."

"What about fiberglass?"

"I don't have a fiberglass tree."

"Very funny, Dad."

I skinned off the bark. Hedge is so full of water that the grain checks badly, and so I dipped the ends in paraffin. Chances are that only one of those pieces will be perfect enough to make a bow. When they are half-dry, I'll rough them out with an ax, then throw them in the attic again.

Sometime around Christmas I'll sculpt the bow. I still have my father's spoke shave.

When the letter arrived in its colored envelope, addressed from Florida in a cramped, precise hand, I was apprehensive. No one writes letters anymore, except to deliver bad news. I threw it on top of the refrigerator to deal with after Dale had gone to bed.

The letter was from Silvie. Otto Sanchez had died, at the VA hospital in Seminole. A drug reaction of some sort, but he'd been failing for several months. I stared at his painting of the vets playing basketball that I'd hung above my desk. It was only then I realized that the guy about to shoot was Otto.

I went outside, past my son and his strange music, and walked to the cabin I use for a utility shed. In a rusted medicine cabinet I keep a pack of Camels. I don't smoke anymore, except once every several months I have three Camels in quick succession—throwing the third away in disgust.

I lay back on a lawn chair and let the smoke tear at my lungs. I looked up at the bright moon, and across the shadowy hills. Oh, to be young again, to meet Trudy for lunch and meander across the campus, talking of how big the world was and how we would change it.

Sometimes, I seem to see Norman in the corner of my eye, when I look across the pasture and spot a tree whose shape is familiar. I saw him last fall when a group of old vets set up the Moving Wall across the field at the elementary school, and one bent low to talk to the second-graders, and muscled up a tattooed arm like mighty Samson.

I think of you, Norman, when I am restless and have gone wandering late at night. I think of you when I'm in Tulsa, and make a little pilgrimage past that Buck Rogers extravaganza, Oral Roberts University. I think of you when I have bad news.

It's good to sleep well, to eat apples you've grown, to study the stars, to move about in fine weather. These are the best ways I know to shake the blues, the feeling that life can't get any worse. It can. Oh, Norman, Norman, my brother, I know it can.

Nathan Mort

JOHN MORT served in Vietnam in 1969 and 1970 as a radio operator with the 1st Cavalry Division. He received his MFA in writing from the University of Iowa in 1974 and his MLS in 1976. The recipient of a National Endowment for the Arts Literature Fellowship in 1992, he is a librarian, columnist, and reviewer whose previous books are the story collections *Tanks* (1987) and *The Walnut King* (1990). He lives in Missouri.